TOO LATE FOR MAN

too late for man
ES TARDE PARA EL HOMBRE

ESSAYS BY
william ospina

TRANSLATED FROM THE SPANISH BY
nathan budoff

BROOKLINE BOOKS

ISBN 1-57129-018-4 (pbk.)

Library of Congress Cataloging-in-Publication Data
Ospina, William, 1954–
   [Es tarde para el hombre. English.]
   Too late for man : essays / by William Ospina : translated from the Spanish by Nathan Budoff.
      120 p.   cm. -- (New Voices from Latin America)
      ISBN 1-57129-018-4 (pbk.)
      I. Budoff, Nathan, 1962–   . II. Title. III. Series.
   PQ8180.25.S63E813   1995
   861--dc20   95-38884
                                 CIP

Cover painting (*The Garden*, 1993) and design by Nathan Budoff. Book design and typography by Erica Schultz.

Published by
BROOKLINE BOOKS
P.O. Box 1047, Cambridge, MA 02238-1047
 PRINTED IN CANADA

contents

introduction

PAUL VALERY DESCRIBED THE TWO GREAT DANGERS WHICH threaten society as two extremes in the same continuum — order and disorder. This text revolves around the order and disorder of contemporary society. It explores one central and recurrent idea: that the kingdom of man may have reached its terminus. The civilization founded on human supremacy, on the idea of the superiority of our species, must yield its place to a more respectful order, an order more amenable to the other creatures.

It also argues that man will only find the road to his own survival if he abdicates his throne of arrogance and discreetly submits to the powers that truly govern life and sustain the universe.

This return to the perception of the divinity of the world could well be what is called for by the complex disorder of this *fin de siècle*. Maybe the terrible power of science, the overwhelming influence of the technological, and the increasingly indiscriminate hostility of man towards his fellow man that we call *military indus-try* and *terrorism*, demonstrate that human supremacy has lost its justification. Maybe they demonstrate that we must search for paths outside of this ingenuous arrogance, that our own fate hangs in the balance, and that because there is something much greater that we now must save, it is too late for man.

From the first of these essays, "The Romantics and the Future," written at the beginning of 1993, all of the others have followed.

— *William Ospina*

... it becomes too evident that, unless this colossal pace of advance can be retarded (a thing not to be expected,) or, which is happily more probable, can be met by counter-forces of corresponding magnitude, forces in the direction of religion or profound philosophy, that shall radiate centrifugally against this storm of life so perilously centripetal towards the vortex of the merely human, left to itself the natural tendency of so chaotic a tumult must be to evil; for some minds to lunacy, for others to a reagency of fleshly torpor.

— THOMAS DE QUINCEY (1845)

It was too late for Man,
But early, yet, for God.
　　　— EMILY DICKINSON

the romantics and the future

BERTRAND RUSSELL ASSERTED THAT THE ULTIMATE MANI-festation of European Romanticism was neither a poem nor a painting, but the death of Byron in Missolonghi, fighting for Greek liberty. He wanted to make it clear that Romanticism was neither a mere pictorial school, nor a poetic or musical moment, but rather a vital attitude, the spirit of a generation of humanity at the end of the eighteenth and the beginning of the nineteenth centuries; a way of relating to the world and our presence in it.

As time distances us from events, they often become clearer. Fifty years ago Hitler could be seen as a fortunate and fanatic military strategist, as an indecipherable mixture of arrogance and ambition. Today, we have begun to see him both as a revival of the cyclical and terrible German vocation of purifying the world (here in Latin America the strange idea of eliminating poverty by killing the poor also arises at times) and as one of the most savage proofs that the nihilism announced by the nineteenth century now flourishes among us.

Romanticism, too, is more clearly visible now — not only as the purest moment of the Western spirit in recent centuries, but also as the solid foundation upon which could be constructed the efforts of our age to find alternatives to the barbarism which is engulfing the planet.

At the end of the eighteenth century, the efforts of intelligence had coalesced into vigorous rational systems. The French Enlightenment, English Empiricism, and German Rationalism had fully developed the cult of reason. There was a faith in human progress and a confidence in the human capacity to comprehend the world and organize it according to human desires. All of the positivism which has imposed itself on the West was nourished by this luminous rationalism. But the principal tendency of positivism is to reduce the vast and complex universal reality to a utilitarian discourse which only accepts demonstrable logic — that which can be calculated, measured, clearly explained in its origins, and expressed in rational formulas. A universe thus reduced is acceptable for the ends of this civilization, dynamized today by the blind force of capital, and pushed forward by profit as the only grand purpose of the species.

If this attitude had been unanimously endorsed by humanity, we would be able to conserve little hope for the future. A world thus reduced to its most obvious manifestations and its most pragmatic mechanisms offers only the death of the human spirit. The detour of humanity into a world of objects without sense, of material without transcendental meaning, results in the confusion of all values and the loss of all purpose. The desanctified world in which we live today, that which is described to us by journalism, that which is sold to us by advertising, that which is offered to us by tourism — that universe explored by science, manipulated by technology, transformed by industry — is gradually being converted into a kingdom of debris where all religion is superfluous, all philosophy excessive, and all poetry frivolous. It is a dizzy and evanescent world where everything is disposable, including human beings, and where the innumerable possible meanings of every object are reduced to one single meaning: its utility.

Thus, as we know, nature has been converted into a bank of resources. The stars are sources of energy, the waters also are sources of energy, the forests are natural resources, all indecipherable material is simply raw material, and human beings are but a labor force. That which the eye encompasses and comprehension grasps — the world which more judicious ages viewed as full of divinities, organized in myths, perpetuated in legends, and celebrated in songs — has become so poor that it is nothing more than a labyrinth without a center, an amalgamation of material without purpose or spirit.

With all the mysterious and confusing excluded,

the world is trapped in the spiderweb of reason, that
great dogmatism which invalidates all discourse that
refuses to yield to its logic of reduction and dissection.
Our lives feel trivial and their passage feels mechanical.
We begin to ask ourselves, what are the great conquests
delivered to our species by the age of rationalism? Is it
really true that in the rational kingdom of merchandise
we are more free than in the empire of the old gods and
their old myths? In the society of consumerism, are we
more opulent? In the kingdom of technology, are we
more peaceful? In the kingdom of reason, are we more
reasonable?

We have passed from the faith in progress which
intoxicated the nineteenth century to a theory of development which casts a few nations into great imperialist
power and many others into subordination and passivity. We are not better than the men of antiquity, but we
have refined our barbarism. There was more innocence and dignity in the advance of Attila's hordes and
Tamerlaine's tartars, who measured their devastating
journeys not by leagues but by degrees of latitude and
longitude, than in the camps of living skeletons and the
gas chambers of the Third Reich.

But the triumph of positivism and the advance of
nihilism are not mere errors or caprices of history. The
end of the Christian era and the crumbling of the values which sustained humanity for centuries, the loss of
a transcendental sense of history, the death of religion
with its guidance and its ethics — these could not help

but precipitate an age of emptiness and confusion. This is how T.S. Eliot has described the process which our culture has followed in this century:

Where is the life we have lost in living?
Where is the wisdom we have lost in knowledge?
Where is the knowledge we have lost in information?
Twenty centuries of human history
Distances us from God and brings us closer to dust.

And Nietzsche's prophetic and lonely outcry portrays our situation starkly: "The desert is growing. / Unfortunate is he who shelters deserts!"

From the end of the nineteenth century, philosophy began to warn us, true to its abilities, that fateful times were drawing nigh. "The most uncomfortable of guests is now at the door," wrote Nietzsche: "Nihilism is now here." Warned of this, we traverse our epoch awaiting the arrival of the terrible guest. Surely we expect a mythological monster, a sort of Leviathan whose eruption will definitively mark the end of time. And though all of us see it, we are slow in recognizing and naming it. Now it is clear where it can be found. Its name is terrorism and drug addiction; it is consumption and advertising; it is narco-trafficking and environmental degradation; it is pornography and statistics; it is the empire of profit and fashion; it is war as an industry; it is the trivialization of both life and death. Marx announced that all things would be converted into merchandise: Today beauty and health are products, learning and celebration are products, and art and knowledge are products. First they sold us earth and fire, today they are selling us water, and tomorrow we will have to pay for air, just as the most asphyxiated already do on the street corners of Tokyo and Mexico.

Each day our relationship with the world is more superfluous and ephemeral. Once water glasses were made so that they would last, so that there would be a meaningful contact between our lives and the mysterious world of objects; today the receptacle lasts not even the time it takes to consume the water it contains. Everything must pass through our hands and disappear immediately, advertising advises us to destroy it at once, in an absurd carnival of evanescence and disrespect for the world. And what is this frenzy of fashion, governed only by the blind impatience of capital, but the triumph of a plethora of hasty masks, of inconstant shadows for which we are not even subjects but barely forms of exhibition? Thus the homes of our consumer society have a tendency to transform themselves into mere terminals of industry — a well-stocked kitchen, closets full of clothes, and in every room, night and day, a television blaring, providing useless and forgettable information to a humanity each day more perplexed and submissive. North American society now approaches this ideal, with its strange passivity and that cult of waste which made the poet Auden exclaim, "The great vice of Americans is not materialism but a lack of respect for matter."

To this same order belongs the considerable acceleration which capital — attentive only to its own reproduction, to the abbreviation of its cycles and the increase of its earnings — has worked on history. We are all agents of this acceleration without being aware of it. Once it was important to learn; today it is important to graduate. Once it was a pleasure to travel; today our only concern is with arriving, and the less you sense and experience the voyage, increasingly associated with a lack of comfort and usefulness, the better. The confinement of humanity in great cities, and their gradual incorporation into this urban rhythm — which lives not only at the margin of nature, but at her expense — seems to be driving our civilization toward a crisis of incalculable proportions. Industry frenetically wastes natural material, frequently in processes which are not reversible. And increasingly, when we look at the phenomena which are the faces of progress and our present condition throughout the world, we feel with alarm that every solution is partial and insufficient, that it is difficult to entrust the business of correcting the course and guaranteeing the future to the nations of the earth, but that neither do private individuals seem capable of detaining, or even altering, this historic tendency.

It is for this reason that I want to linger in a consideration of Romanticism. This movement, the largest and most complex Western spiritual movement in re-

cent centuries, arose, as is common knowledge, as a
reaction to triumphant rationalism. It was because light
inundated all spheres of human activity that Novalis
wrote "The Hymns of the Night," the clarion call of
Romanticism. His intention was clear. What sensible
creature, asked Novalis, doesn't love light above all
things, that divine clarity which fills and clarifies all
things? Yet he quickly adds: "But I return toward the
mysterious and ancient night, owner of a more profound power." He then starts to celebrate the gifts of
the night, all of that which remains in the darkness of
the inexpressible and the inscrutable. From slightly
before this moment, but especially thenceforth, Romanticism extended its dark blanket over Europe and
America, and assumed the responsibility of reminding
us of the existence of a reality much more vast than
that into which positivism locked us. Reason could exclude from its discourse, and even from consideration,
all that which was not clearly explicable in its origin,
measurable in its extension, predictable in its function
and definable in terms of rational formulas. But — although we know not how to explain or measure them,
how to anticipate or control them — pain and illness
exist; terror and imagination, love, insanity and death
exist; hopes and premonitions, dreams and deliriums,
the divine and the demoniac exist. Thus the Romantics
undertook not only the recovery, but the exaltation of
this world of passions and mysteries that constitutes for
man the inextricable fabric of reality. For triumphant

positivism, all that was not quantifiable could be slippery; in terms of statistics, dead people could disappear into mortality indices, and people destroyed by society and misery could disappear into poverty indices. But the real world is full of real pain and real terror, of nightmares more intense and memorable than any action, and of dramas more hazardous and inexplicable than any nightmare. When the windows and air holes began to swing closed to the spirit, the Romantics forced open not only the gates to the fields where immortal nature, full of miracles, continued breathing, but also the portals and the trapdoors to the unexplored basements of consciousness, tunnels and passages that the world no longer wanted to acknowledge.

Some would say that it is a benevolent act to exclude from the world all that we have been unable to comprehend and all that we know not how to control. But monsters do not disappear because we turn our glance away from them. The pretension of positivism to banish the dark, the confusing and the inexplicable by means of what philosophers call the *Praecisio Mundi* (the precision of the world) — the adoption of a language which ignores all that can't be reasoned — is similar to the pathetic reaction of a scared child who decides to close his eyes so as not to see the darkness of the night. Here is the real triumph of rationalism, and there is something here which belongs not to the realm of prudence, civility and clarity, but to the overflowing of the passions and, we almost feel tempted to say, to the unchaining of the demons. In fact, it seems that a collection of mysterious forces has taken possession of history, and the wise men who preached and professed reason are conferring and debating, asking themselves from whence comes all this clamor? If the fantastic divine figures were now under control, what could these be? And we seem to hear the voice of Novalis (that exquisite and astonishing young man, who died at 29 years of age, leaving the world bewildered) exclaiming from the twilight of the eighteenth century that "in the absence of gods, phantoms reign."

Romanticism, of course, was not a system, nor was it faithful to any program. It sprang from that same dark background from which spring the great problems and great solutions of the species. It was an epoch of passion and exaltation, of imagination and rhythm. It was a strange whirlwind which elevated a multitude of fervent and brilliant youths to the heights of inspiration and heroism, and then plunged them again into their murky coffins. That bit of darkness which they snatched from the sky was paid for at a very high price, and humanity may not be aware of this offering which the romantic generations gave to them.

Nobody has yet explained well why the Romantics died so young, nonetheless leaving behind splendid works, more memorable and even at times much more extensive than those of men who reached maturity and old age. In France, in England, and in

Germany — the same countries where Reason had
prospered — the voices, the music, the images and
the forms of this new sensibility began to rise up,
upset by a sudden sense of evanescence and wonder, full of an impetuous mysticism in the face of the
gravity and enormity of nature, tending toward a
nostalgia for more naïve ages, ages more filled with
energy and faith. Keats, entranced in the celebration of the solitary song of the nightingale in the night
forest, heard there the hymn of the immortality of
the species; he stopped to listen to the silent voice of
the dead ages, which still leave promises in the friezes
that skirt ceremonial urns. Shelley used the voice of
the elements to call for the rebellion and renovation
of the times. Wordsworth made a great effort to fill
the present with a transcendental feeling and to my-
thologize the landscape. Byron transformed his whole
life into a dramatic succession of passion and music.
Victor Hugo constructed his great verbal monuments.
Gerard de Neyval read in the signs of his times not
only the evidence of a great poverty, the solitude that
the death of great dreams had left in the spirit, and
the memory of having been in beautiful towers and
siren's grottoes, but also the arrival of the frame of
mind that announces the return of a sacred order.
Novalis alternated the vindication of darkness with
the editing of a fragmentary encyclopedia of prophetic ideas. Hölderlin closed the enormous task with
his invocation of a return to the sacred, his invita-

tion to a holy alliance with nature, and his recovery of the role of the poet as messenger of the divine.

The Romantics also turned a new gaze over the past. Where the classicists had seen ornamental cultures (as in Greece) or epochs of darkness (as in the Middle Ages), the Romantic generation discovered a treasury of unknown cultures, new aesthetic propositions, and forgotten beauties and terrors. Winkelmann had rediscovered Greece. He had encountered the shadowy, turbulent and orgiastic side of the culture which would later be called Dionysian. Hölderlin, his great disciple, proposed to the world a version of Greece where the gods were not, as Schiller had thought, "beautiful figures of the land of mythology," but powers, spiritual states, truths and destinies.

The Romantics understood that Greece — let us describe it with a phrase from Rubén Darío: "Was judged to be marble but was live flesh." And only through this discovery could Hölderlin have a presentiment of those future divinities which are the heart of his poetry.

But above all Romanticism was about cracking the surface of reason and its skepticism. It was the same time when the Grimm brothers were dedicating themselves to the recovery of the great medieval saga, the fairy tales — a spontaneous expression of the collective spirit in an age of great spiritual conflicts. From one glance over the incalculable wealth of the Middle Ages — with its heretics and witches, its castles and kings, its legends of chivalry and its perfect damsels, its witches'

Sabbaths and its mystics; with its libraries full of specters and its nights full of demons, with its crusaders
and its liturgical songs, with its lechery and its Gothic
cathedrals, with its Julian Hospitalario and its Francis
of Assisi, with the crystal skies of Dante and the peni-
tential infernos of the Holy Acts — the imagination of
Romanticism nourished itself. Everything served to be
recreated: Tristan and Isolde, Sigmund's broken sword,
the avaricious dragons of the north, the dialogues of
St. Joan with the forests of Domrémy, and those innumerable creatures: angels, witches, elves, unicorns, gob-
lins and sylphs, monsters, hydras, demons, naiads,
nymphs, chimeras, specters, gnomes, giants, and will-
o'-the-wisps. These creatures, today trivialized by commerce, were treated by those men with a shocking intensity: they *believed* in them, as creatures and as sentiments, as incarnations of terror or wonder. Reading a
story as beautiful and delicate as "Ondina," by Friedrich
de La Motte-Fouque, or the stories of Hoffman, you
can feel that these things disturbed and terrified their
authors; that unlike today, they were not trivial con-
ventions of consumerism developed by impassive manu-
facturers.

There are few men as emblematic of Romanticism
as Edgar Allen Poe, whose intoxicated and hallucina-
tory figure tends to stick in one's memory. Borges re-
counts that when Poe was accused of imitating Hoffman's
stories, he answered, "Horror isn't from Germany, it's
from the soul." Novalis could have said the same thing

about beauty, Beethoven about passion, William Turner about bewilderment, Caspar Davis Friedrich about reverence, Whitman about enthusiasm, and Hölderlin about divinity. Compared to the Surrealists, who rarely escaped the routine of commerce and the defiant gesture, the Romantics profoundly marked their epoch, infecting the multitudes with their dreams and their imaginations. They were the soul of the world, and they had an enduring influence on the mental habits and the sensibilities of the people.

But the world advanced — or retreated — to more arid regions. Today we can think that Romanticism was an epoch, but more than anything it was an omen. We can compare it, as in Milton's verse, to the first buds of spring which are destroyed by the last winds of winter: the presentiment of the future silenced by the forces of tradition. But, some will ask, how could an age so bent on nostalgia, so drunk on ancient visions — an age that seemed to want to go backwards at every moment, a hyper-aesthetic and insomniacal age, full of dark youths, fevers and nightmares — be similar to the future? What could an age so shadowed by the Middle Ages, so moved by ruins, so confused by fantasies, promise for the yet-to-come? Doesn't it seem more like illness than health? Doesn't it speak more of pessimism than hope?

Maybe it is there that one encounters the principal secret of Romanticism. There is no time of life when there is more crying and more fever than in childhood;

there is no time that is more agitated by terrors, more impressionable and more gullible. And yet, there is no greater vitality than that of childhood. This gullibility, which is a form of innocence, could be healthier than the skepticism and suspicion which characterize our times. Today we are compelled to believe only in the evidence, but the evidence is no more than an illusion. We are obligated to disbelieve in miracles, and nonetheless, the only thing in which one can believe is a miracle. Our problem is that we are too sensible, too sane, too precise.

Something has been taken from us, and that something is our astonishment before unexplainable reality. It would astonish us to see a boulder float, but it would not astonish us to see the planet float. It would make us uneasy if a house was never finished, but it doesn't seem to make us uneasy that the universe may have no end. It seems to us that an object, or phenomenon, stops being mysterious once it is disguised in mathematical formulas. And this reminds me of one of Chesterton's reflections that "against those who affirm that the universe was miraculously created from nothing, the modern scientific theory is raised, which demonstrates that it wasn't a sudden act but a slow and gradual process of evolution and increasing complexity of the material." And then Chesterton asks us: "Whose idea was it that a miracle stops being a miracle if it is diffused over time?"

The fundamental characteristic of the Romantics is

not their choice of themes but their attitude. In this
Bertrand Russell is correct. Romanticism was a vital
attitude, an age of dreams and ideals; its men were not
satisfied with watching the movement of the markets or
the news of the world, they had a "Hunger for space
and a thirst for heaven." They had an anxiety for eternity, and they were infinitely capable of dreaming, of
believing and of delivering their lives to these dreams.
Byron believed in liberty, and for this dream he died at
thirty-six years of age in the swamps of Missolonghi.
Keats believed in beauty; to this dream he gave his life,
and his verse is filled with this faith. At the end of the
"Ode on a Grecian Urn," he tells us:

> *Beauty is truth, truth beauty; that is all*
> *Ye know on earth, and all ye need to know.*

And in another of his poems he lays the foundation
of this virtual religion of beauty which he has proposed:

> *A thing of beauty is a joy forever.*

I don't know if it would be accurate to insist that
this age of reason is the age of disillusion. It would
certainly require many drugs to produce in man an
enthusiasm comparable to that which a faith or a cause
can produce. Man is a very small being when he does
not have a purpose, when he is reduced to a solitary

and passive consumer made lethargic by the ideal of comfort.

After the long journey of modern society, with its urgency and its machines, with its utilitarianism and its efficiency, with its industrial drugs that alleviate pain and its industrial cities that induce illness, with its cults of youth, health and beauty that in reality tend toward desperation and fascism, with its frenetic supermarkets and its spectacles; after the long journey which has brought us to this disquieting and always frustrated greed for intense pleasures that is known as *drug addiction*, to this blind conflict between social arbitrariness and individual randomness that is known as *terrorism*, to this positivist kingdom of sex deprived of all spirituality and sold as merchandise that is known as *pornography*, to this abandonment of being — at the same time bored and hungry — that we know as *consumer society*, we return to the Romantics to discern in them our lost magnificence. "Here is a man," Napoleon is said to have exclaimed in a drawing room in Weimar, indicating counselor Wolfgang von Goethe. And this is what men of today exclaim looking at those passionate dreamers, all lucidity and all passion, who understood that reason is an essential element for prevailing in the world, but that it cannot be the foundation of our relationship with the world.

"Man is a god when he dreams / and only a beggar when he thinks," wrote Hölderlin at the beginning of his "Hyperion." And so that no one should think that he — disciple of Fichte, passionate conversationalist with Hegel and Schelling in his classroom in Tübingen, thoughtful reader of Kant and Plato — was merely disdainful of intelligence, or someone who neglected the importance of thought, in a poem about Socrates and Alcibiades he wrote, "He who has thought the most deeply / loves with the most life."

In this sense, reason cannot be a final criterion for appraisal of the world. For when it is completely used up and leaves us evidence that we never fully knew the meaning, the origin, the composition and the purposes of the universe, we will still always have a love for life, stronger and more full of gratitude in proportion to the inexplicable nature of being. And there, in the place where wind gets tired, where reason encounters its limits, there the divine begins, and the function of art is to reveal it, make us sensitive to its presence and its influence, enliven our gratitude.

This is the function which the Romantics fulfilled: to renovate, at the beginning of the modern age, the vital ties which unite us to the mysterious, to the divine and to immortal nature — and to leave floating above the winds, once the deserts of utilitarianism and lack of sense had grown, a memory of noble destinies and an example of audacious adventures, so that something sacred and powerful could present itself as an option in the hour of great eclipses.

Now we need dreams and goals. The evils which reign over civilization, and which grow without respite each day, demand audacious solutions and original destinies. We as yet know not what countenances the divine will assume in the times to come. We still do not know the text of the new laws which will be needed to insure our survival and our liberty. But of all the innumerable generations of humanity, only we are here, facing this challenge. Now both Christianity and positivism, with their theories of vague luminous futures, have failed to seduce man into accepting his present poverty. But, as Whitman said,

There was never any more inception than there is
*   now,*
Nor any more youth or age than there is now,
And will never be any more perfection than there is
*   now,*
Nor any more heaven nor hell than there is now.

It is here, in these streets and on these corners, where history awaits our answer and life awaits our findings.

I want to make a final consideration. We, the children of this region of the world, have always been taught to see history as something distant and foreign. We could claim as ours Rimbaud's statement: "True life is absent, / we are not in the world."

History was an affair of prestigious peoples and illustrious civilizations. From the shore we watched the distant fireworks and shipwrecks, we heard the din of battle, and we surrendered ourselves to its results. But suddenly now, in the savage times of nihilism, history has begun to walk our streets; we are not distant witnesses but protagonists and victims of the great dramas of our times. Now we cannot leave the search for paths for humanity in the hands of others. All of us know, now without the slightest doubt, that the danger is here. And our only choice is to believe in the validity of those verses written by Hölderlin: "There where danger grows / Salvation also grows."

the pitfalls of progress

IT IS SAID THAT WHEN SIGMUND FREUD HEARD THAT HIS BOOKS were being burned by the Nazis, he exclaimed, "Look how the world has advanced; in the Middle Ages they would have burned *me*!" In reality, the world had not advanced; millions entered the ovens of fascism, to be converted into ashes, and many others walk on forever scarred and deformed by the humiliation and degradation practiced by that singularly modern ideology. The words of Freud remain instead an ironic commentary on his era, as well as on the way the world has left behind the hell of the Second World War, and tried to purify itself of its evils by incarnating them in a few horrible demons.

The nineteenth century — good child of the Renaissance, the Enlightenment and the other rationalisms — had erected progress as the great faith of modern times. If there was one thing which gave no quarter to either doubt or criticism, it was the evidence that the world was now progressing. Servitude was better than slavery; salaried work was better than servitude. And in the background of these ever-diminishing sufferings was insinuated the paradise of brotherly society, the last step in a progression which had uprooted us from the animal condition and elevated us into the superior species — administrators, like the Egyptian lords of marble, "of the gifts of heaven, earth and the Nile." Humans were creatures superior to nature. Now liberated by reason, we could feel, as did Hamlet, "In action how like an angel! in apprehension how like a god!"

It is true that there seems to be a contradiction between the incessant character of progress in the past and the expectation of a happy ending which would make the same progress finally unnecessary. Once the ideal society was achieved, where would we progress? But happiness is not an object of criticism. There remains far too much misfortune in the world; all of these questions can wait until later, until afterward.

The idea of progress was the light of the nineteenth century. All believed in it, from the foolish to the wise. Hegel was its standard bearer; the cannons of the French Revolution were its reveille. Science was charged with opening and amplifying its perspectives, technology with deepening them, and industry with making them more evident to the populace. Who could deny that never before had so many things been discovered, had so many things been invented, had the world changed so much?

Of course the idea of progress was not new. There

has never been an ideology in history which has not presented itself as the great conquest that replaces and overwhelms all others. Christianity had replaced the ungodliness of the pagan cults, and the solitary objections of Julian the Apostate were of no consequence. The dream of the Great Empire replaced the intimate and dispersed villages of the Middle Ages. The Aristotelian thinking of Thomas Aquinas replaced the spirituality of Augustine. The age of discoveries had broadened the horizons of war, and the discovery of America had completed the new idea of the world. More than that, the conquest of America was the perfect measure for Western civilization to confirm its sensation that not only did progress exist, but that they were its guide and instigator. Progress and development were what the civilized nations brought to the good and bad savages of the new lands of God.

History had nourished those certainties, and the eighteenth century completed their affirmation. It thus feels a bit strange that the whirlwinds of light at times hoisted up certain dark clouds. In contrast to the optimism of the Enlightenment, which was to be the intellectual core of the French Revolution, we find that phrase of Voltaire's: "We leave the world as evil and stupid as we found it upon arriving."

Also in contrast to all this reason is the spirit of Swedenborg, who — after being a worshipper of the sciences, and an instrument of progress and progress's wars — drifted toward the intemporality of mysticism and toward the complex postulation of a universal ethics.

But these lucidities and doubts could not contain the impetus of the times, and the arrival of the Industrial Revolution definitively installed progress on one of the most stable thrones of the modern age. Even Romantics like Victor Hugo believed in it and exalted it. Everyone who had suffered an affront in tradition could find their vindication and vengeance in progress. All would change; nothing, luckily, would be as before. It was Rimbaud who said, "One must be absolutely modern." It is very possible that he actually thought his poetry was a real manifesto of modernity, a progress that left behind the "*vielles enormités crevées*" of the classics. But to think that there is progress in art, in music, or in poetry is simply one of the most prolonged and damaging errors of criticism. Some really believe that a work can be rejected for not being modern, while others think that it can be rejected for being modern. These attitudes displace the aesthetic discussion to a plane which is too unreal. What gives a work its value is not its temporality but its *intemporality*, its capacity to make sense to peoples of many different cultures and many different eras. If today somebody wrote like Homer or like Dante, they would have to be accepted and appreciated, as the aesthetic value of a work corresponds to its internal truth, to its organic coherence, and is not based on any exterior condition. As Borges explained so well, the self-styled *modern* poems of Apollinaire

now seem antiquated to us, while the glimpses and
sentiments of Rilke (a man who never presented himself as modern) continue to seem contemporary — that
is, eternal.

There is no progress in art. The drawings of Picasso
are not *superior to* nor *more advanced than* those that
the visitor to Altamira painted on the wall. Molière is
not superior to Sophocles, nor Rodin to Phidias. Each
work of art proposes its own ideal, establishes its own
level of excellence and neither refutes nor replaces other
works. This is not only reasonable, but just. To suggest
that the people of the twentieth century better perceive
the beauty of the world, better capture its strangeness,
and necessarily celebrate it better, than people of other
eras is almost like arguing that the roses of New York
are better than the roses of Persepolis. It is like arguing
for a cosmic discrimination, a sort of multiplying beati-
tude at the expense of the past.

The theory of evolution is one of the roots of this
idea of progress in art. In its current form, evolution
is interpreted as a continual process of purification
and improvement over the previous states of material and nature. Although we all know that the monu-
mental community of the dinosaurs was erased from
the face of the earth very quickly, we still speak of
the survival of the fittest in the fight for life. But what
the theory seems to suggest is that all of these previous states of nature and life were frustrated attempts
in the search for the perfection that the human spe-

cies today believes itself to embody.

It is certain that for centuries our religions and philosophies played with the notion that we were astral travelers stopping over on the planet. Unlike rocks, we had senses. Unlike plants, we could move autonomously. Unlike the beasts, we had intelligence and language. Unlike the savage tribes — who were evidently animals — we had souls. All of our efforts for centuries were directed toward differentiating ourselves from the world, and this allowed us to work like foreign magicians, very distant from the monkeys whom we resemble so much and very akin to the angels whom we resemble so little.

Thus, when we started to accept that we pertained to the earth, our principal preoccupation seems to have become explaining why we were different and better, and evolution arose as the perfect formula for accepting our origins while also confirming our superiority. Every difference supposes the superiority of humanity. The ant might be more hard-working and foresighted than man, but man was superior because he was bigger and stronger. The elephant might be bigger and stronger, but man was superior for whatever reason was opportune: intelligence, ingenuity, cunning — maybe even for being more hard-working and foresighted.

But does evolution, in reality, imply progress? Are wings superior to fins? Are lungs superior to gills? Is man better than other species? Until just a few decades ago, not only would the answers have been affirmative, but the very questions would have seemed ridiculous. Today the suspicion that our species is the most dangerous plague which the planet has begotten has us submerged in a mysterious stupor, and no one dares guess what path civilization will take.

There are those who affirm, nonetheless, that the species — greedy, covetous, fratricidal and savage — persisted through millennia in its conflicts and its struggles without ever endangering the foundations of the world and the order of the universe. And that it is only the exaltation of human knowledge, the triumph of reason, science, technology and industry, which has put us in a condition to not only destroy civilization, but to drag down all of magic and innocent nature in our shipwreck.

Running like bucks across the surface of the earth, excavating its innards like moles, submerging ourselves in its depths like fish, soaring in the planetary air like birds, and — unlike any other creatures — pushing out beyond the atmosphere, man has taken on all other beings in the domain of this world; he has made the whole world his kingdom. It is astonishing to see how we not only feed ourselves with every creature but also ride the strongest colts, govern the enormous elephants from their backs, drive vast flocks, direct herds of buffalo, and receive the prisoners which falcons bring from the sky. In our circuses we make ferocious tigers leap calmly through burning hoops of fire, make enormous bears dance pirouettes on colored balloons, and convert friendly monkeys into distressing caricatures of people.

In all of this there is ingenuity, industriousness and an evident capacity for domination. But there is also a great margin of indifferent cruelty, of disrespect for a mysterious order which has always treated us with the fundamental loyalty of one who submits himself to invariable laws. In the background of our intelligence, a dense cloud of stupidity makes us almost always use our ingenuity for atrocious designs. There is a strange pleasure in dominating others, whether animals or humans; there is, Montaigne said, "a point of bittersweet voluptuousness" in provoking another's suffering. And at the same time, the creatures' docility, innocence, and passivity can be viewed as proof that they deserve to be dominated. It seems that man is incapable of respecting that which does not put up resistance and those who do not practice violence. Thus humanity only adopted the pacifist doctrine of Christ after applying to its promulgator the necessary punishment of the cross. And, in a very human maneuver, this same Christian doctrine later served to disguise and conceal the worst cruelties, the most intolerant and merciless wars.

But man, who has been able to dominate the world and subjugate his peers, does not seem to have power over himself. His inventions have now acquired an irresistible force and seem to be no longer governed by the will of their creator. Man has stirred up powers which he seems to be in no condition to dominate. The fable of the sorcerer's apprentice related in Goethe's poem, which we enjoyed in an animated film fifty years ago, today seems to be taking on the weight of a gigantic tragedy.

Now it is less evident than before that man is the superior creature of nature, that his place is to be the dominator and the king. Now it is less evident that all evolution really is evolution, that is to say, an improvement. Now it is less evident that certain types of differences among the species imply some kind of superiority and authorize domination, depredation and termination of the others. In the natural order, evolution merely represents the modification and adaptation of beings to different conditions, but it doesn't seem to ascend toward the formation of a superior type of being — and even if it does, man does not appear to be the miraculous offspring of this large and troubled process.

But the modern mentality assumes that man is the perfect creature; that everything must define itself in relation to him; that the planet is his warehouse of unlimited and inexhaustible resources; that the future is the stage of his exclusive comfort and happiness; that all orders of life owe him submission and tribute; that all material is unrestrictedly offered to him; and what is more, that the illusion of natural progress has been converted into the foundation of another illusion — the illusion that everything in history is governed by the law of progress.

Thus every invention of modernity arrives sanctified by the idea that all novelty is implicitly an advance. No one doubts that today's cars are better than yesterday's cars; few consider that the proliferation of automobiles represents an exchange of pride and comfort for the oxygen of the planet and the right to the ozone layer.

Apparently we owe gratitude to the forces constructing our gallows. It seems that we are obliged to shout "Viva progress!" every time a new silliness or a new atrocity appears. If the vertigo of fashion chains the youth of the world to a frenetic servitude; if the cities of the world grow without control or planning, dazzling new immigrants with promises each day more false; if to save the output of capital, pesticides poison the countryside; if the military industries work day and night to produce ever more sophisticated instruments of death; if without reflection we transform the materials of the world into inert substances incapable of returning to the natural cycle; if we multiply the monstrous non-biodegradable debris, "Viva progress!" If technology and industry impose a constantly more wild and urgent rhythm in our lives, in our work, in our travels, in our pleasure, in our music, a rhythm which excludes the divine and soon will exclude the human, "Viva progress!" If the dictatorial universe of advertising invades our space and our minds without respite; if schools continue substituting an antiquated and authoritarian

discourse for a live relationship with the world, usurp-
ing the space of discovery and learning; if the idle inventions of technology make us each day more passive,
more sedentary and more immobile; if the mania of
specialization leaves us each day more defenseless in
the hands of technicians each day more obtuse; if science explores the entrails of reality and threateningly
manipulates the universe of the gods without respect
and without scruples, "Viva progress!"

Now there is no limit to the inventions and creations which want to impose themselves using this
path. I suppose that once upon a time things had to
prove their utility before they were accepted; now it
seems sufficient if someone announces them as something new and someone sells them as something ad-
vantageous. Thus it is that we have been invaded,
and not always in a transitory manner, by things
which any sensible mind would reject if the itch of
novelty didn't inhibit reflection. We still see over there,
depressing and sinister, the plastic vegetation that
fascinated people just a few decades ago. There must
have been more than a few who believed that finally
progress had given us flowers and plants that didn't
need to be watered and cared for. We still see that
milky and spectral lighting that covers every space
with the sadness of a hospital or a jail.

The diversity of peoples and cultures also tends to
be erased by the rise of an international culture of jeans,
t-shirts and Chiclets; a culture of homogenous com-

mercial molds, of massive planetary spectacles, of identical news. Every day it replaces curious and rich traditions — complex costumes pregnant with meanings, potions, legends, a plentiful and profound universe rooted a thousand different ways in the nutritious earth — with only one lonely expression which is almost always trivial and evanescent.

Like officers in an army, capital enjoys erasing differences and making men appear uniform. When we are no longer these millions of singular faces — each expressing a past, a character and a soul — but the same being, stupidly and infinitely repeated, this curious modern tendency which is called progress will have reached its plenitude. This progress toward losing all of the conquests of civilization, toward diluting in a few imposed colors the infinite variety of shades of the human spirit. Thus we complete the melancholy vision of those verses of Emerson, according to which man will decline, "Star by star his world resigning."

It is possible that a few inventions of the age could generate, for their novelty or their practicality, the illusion of real progress. Constantly better and faster airplanes can generate the illusion of an immense power over the distances and the kingdoms — but we should remember that men like Alexander and Marco Polo lived the adventure of the world better than the rushed executives of today, going each day from an identical airplane to an identical hotel room and from there to an identical conference room, confined within a world which they now feel no need to explore since they already know the statistics. I also think of those athletic Asian tourists who hurriedly descend from buses to take their turn in front of the camera standing by the corresponding building or statue, and who rapidly leave with the plunder of memorable photographs which some other day will tell them where they were.

For beings possessed by the illness of production, machines that abbreviate the processes must be great progress. For musicians whose work demands more and more pieces, and more profit, a machine which replaces twenty instruments and their respective players with one computer program must be progress. Nobody seems to deplore that along the road of progress the ancient delight of making things has gotten lost. That same music used to include twenty different manners of producing harmonious sounds, the voices sprouting from wood and metal, the tints that are added by the spirits of each player as they play these beautiful objects. To leave out the richness of the processes — the pleasure which they provoke, the benevolent effect which the slow elaboration of things works on the spirit — and prefer only the rapidity of the results: to this apex of renunciation have the times brought us. There are those who prefer listening to recordings than live voices; those who would rather watch small figures of light act out predictable dramas on the screen than converse with flesh-and-blood people, with their disquieting and unpredictable humanity.

But the mockery of the modern idea of progress is better undressed in certain apparently minute details: the increase in things which save physical and mental energy; the rise of a culture of waste that invests the efforts of thousands of beings in things whose function is to endure an instant, things which are marked by their duty to immediately wear out, things whose use can't be repeated. A melancholy plastic cup would be the perfect symbol of this superficial and squandering age if the two symbolic crutches of our decline weren't competing with it — these being the portable calculator, without which we're now incapable of adding up the minutes we have saved using it, and the polyhedral remote control, which has brought our domestic immobility to levels of unsuspected perfection.

If progress necessarily existed, the world would not have grown from the century of Hadrian to the century of Hitler, from the universal mind of Francis of Assisi to those monstrous tables with elephant feet that they exhibit in certain decorative stores, from the genocide of Genghis Khan to the genocide of Pol Pot. To advance and retreat in capricious waves seems to have been the fate of the human species, strangely detached from the natural order as the owner of the world and referee and executioner of the life forms. But this idea that progress is something evident and necessary especially stunts our ability to think about the possibility of some real progress — that is, the fruit of effort and not of inertia, of foresight and not of fatalism.

Until very recently, the division of the world into *developed* and *developing* nations made visible the idea of a linear advance which, with the investment of sufficient effort and sufficient self-denial, would carry our undeveloped nations to the splendor of industrialization, opulence and culture. Today the expression "developing" could be more of a threat than a promise, but the sad truth is that the world is one and the seeds of the catastrophe are widely distributed. The general monotony of the scheme of life in the rich societies, with its limited options of work and consumption, drugs and superstition, passivity and spectacle, has its correlation in the prostration of the multitudes in the poor societies with their growing numbers of homeless, their excluded majorities, and their rising violence and crime. Each planetary phenomenon has at least two faces: while in the north it is called *disposability*, in the south it is called *indigence*; and what in the north is known as *drug addiction*, in the south is reflected as *drug trafficking*; and what the north produces in *military industry*, in the south is used in *guerrilla warfare*. But at the very least it is now evident that there are not two worlds and even less three, but only one, and that every effort to resolve certain people's problems without considering the problems of the others can be only stupidity or malice.

If the picture we see today on our planet is the expression of progress that was announced by the prophets of the nineteenth century, one would have to say that the world has progressed too much, and that any deviation or retreat seems preferable to continuing to press further into these shadowy territories. What apparently awaits us in the future could surpass even the highly pessimistic forecasts of science fiction. The labyrinths of functionaries described by Stanislaw Lem, the cosmic desecrations of the space expeditions in Bradbury's work, and the omnipotent corporations and gloomy proletariat of Frederick Pohl's visions are small threats next to the promises of various real planetary Mafia. Every day we are threatened by the black market of nuclear weapons, the proliferation of radioactive residues, and the teratological warehouses of genetic engineering.

Could mere lucidity, now as we stand on the threshold of a new millennium, detain the unrestricted race of the stallions of progress? Maybe it wouldn't be impossible if humanity observed that behind the seductions of advertising, the merchandise of industry, the wonders of science and the marvels of technology hides something monstrous and impassive, which by flattering man, preaching his comfort and supremacy, spurs him toward his ruin. But we are too besieged by temptations, too absorbed in our video monitors, too astounded by acts and objects, too pursued by necessity or by the rush to possess; and in the meantime, loyal to the world that they measure, the watches run more quickly each day.

the song of the sirens

LIKE BUDDHA'S FATHER, CONTEMPORARY SOCIETY SEEMS determined to prevent its children from noticing the existence of sickness, old age and death. At least in the West, a near-religion of health, youth and beauty is spreading, in contrast to the increasingly damaging character of industry, the increasingly lethal character of science, and the increasingly brutal character of the economy. The principal instrument of this cult is advertising, which on a daily basis sells us an image of the world without most of the negative, dangerous and disturbing elements of reality. Beautiful and happy athletic youths populate this universe of paper and light where nobody suffers tragedies which can't be resolved with the proper product; where nobody ages if they use the appropriate face cream; where nobody gets fat if they drink the correct beverage; where nobody is alone if they buy the perfumes or cigarettes or cars which are recommended; where nobody dies if they consume well. This curious paradise of well-being, beauty and com-

fort may not have a parallel in the history of world
religions, which always derived at least part of their
power from reminding humanity of their limitations
and their pathetic destiny. But I dare to think that even
the most despotic and undesirable religions were en-
gaged in saving man — were sincere even in their errors
and deviations. This opulent contemporary religion is
no more than the infinitely seductive mask of an inhuman power which ostentatiously despises man and the
world and does not even know it. This strange power
has discovered what Schopenhauer described: that the
destiny of man is no more than a chain of constantly
renewable appetites; a yearning which never encounters its definitive satiation, an endless chase round and
round on the wheel of imagined need and illusory sat-
isfaction. But this discovery, which could bring the
philosopher to propose the absolute valorization of the
moment, the celebration of the ephemeral and the exaltation of desire which "always begins again" as in
Valery's ocean, has compelled industry to take advantage of the human condition for the brutal designs of a
blind and deaf accumulation. The values which humanity exalted for centuries as ideal or especially pleasant forms of its existence — youth, health, beauty and
vigor — end up being used as lures to induce humanity
to a constantly more artificial and unjustified consumption. We see those beautiful girls who vacillate along
that most tempting of borderlines, between modesty
and licentiousness; we see those androgynous youths

who copy the gestures of classical marble statues; we see those couples who look surprised as they are captured on the thresholds of love and desire. Everything is temptation and sensuality; all of these bodies are offered at the same time, as promises and as paradigms of a full and happy life in which the ritual will never cease: a world where abundance has no pauses, where love does not vacillate, where vitality never tires and beauty never blinks, in its studied eternity of photographs and commercial films. And it seems to us that there is an army of beings working for our happiness. Homeopathic magic actually works: we come to feel that the soft drink will make us younger, the exercise bicycle will make us perfect, and certain foods will make us immortal. Our daily existence, full of imperfections, voids, and lonelinesses, seems for a moment to touch the uncontaminated kingdom of the archetypes. But consumption passes, and life continues its combustion and erosion. Our appetites are reborn, and we don't manage to understand why there is something in us which feels increasingly unsatisfied, something which seems each day more contemptible and more defeated. Perhaps we will never be that beautiful, although we buy everything they sell us; perhaps we will never be that healthy, that calm, that successful, that admired, that wealthy. The illusions which oblige us to buy reveal themselves as inaccessible, but in the end we find the defect not in the opulent archetypes but in our own imperfection.

This seduction takes us by surprise even though we are aware that beauty, like all involuntary virtues, is suspicious. Once it was easier to know where beauty resided. We learned it from Greek marble statues and from European art; its canons were established; they corresponded to the image of the dominant races of civilization. Faced with these models, the Africans were apelike, the Asians pale, ugly and small, the Native Americans crude and grotesque, mulattos deformed and mestizos simple and trivial. But Nazism definitively unmasked the error of thinking that certain physical characteristics bear some kind of morphological, intellectual, or moral superiority. We have seen the most famously civilized nations of the world profess ridiculous theories and support crimes founded on the most inept speculations. And we have learned various things: that the pure races with their ideals of beauty are no more than geographic curiosities; that the increasing crossbreeding and blending of all peoples makes beauty something much more ample, diverse and variable; and that beauty itself, with all its power over culture, must be subordinated to ethics and cannot be glorified as an absolute and autonomous principle. I believe that today we can affirm that every cult of physical beauty carries within it several drops of the most dangerous fascisms.

And it is in exactly this way that advertising uses beauty toward its own ends. The faces and bodies which it offers us are bait. When we think we have bitten into the brilliant salmon, we realize that it was nothing more than the mask of the tapered fishhook, and once again we have fallen for the trick.

Novalis affirmed that "in the absence of the gods, phantoms rule." Perhaps in no other age of human history have there been as many phantoms as in this industrial society, papered as it is with icons — where multitudes spend their days and nights listening to voices of the living and the dead which are in reality grooves in acetate and bands of tape; desiring living and dead beings who are in reality ink stains, incapable of satisfying the desires they provoke; and watching the lives of living and dead creatures who are in reality light rays. The worst part is that each day we look at each other less, because these dizzying glass cubes are more interesting and at the same time demand nothing more from us than complacence and passivity. Books make demands on our imagination; they were made for creative beings, while the arts of contemporary technology only saturate and stun. Thus the beautiful phantom can burst into them at any moment, the serpent of capital with a juicy apple in its mouth, something that no reader would tolerate and that all of us would understand as a maddening intrusion.

Advertising also purifies and refines. It took quite a bit of work to convince businessmen to replace those dull, dictatorial and obscene messages which invaded homes with beautiful, cordial and subtle messages whose orders are both more pleasant and more effective. The sirens of capital sing a little more sweetly each day, and now there are those who think that the true art of our age is in these automobile advertisements which show, not steering wheels or levers or valves, but a willow leaf skidding across the surface of a lake to the rhythm of lilting music. These idyllic fragments of nature are branded in some corner with the unforgettable logo, exactly the same way the slave was branded with his owner's mark. The symbol is there to remind us that what they are showing us does not exist by itself; to remind us that the purpose of the message is not to invite us out for a gentle ride in the country, but to suggest the purchase of an automobile — to remind us who is the owner.

Very few would not agree that the language of advertising is one of the most authoritarian languages. The imperative forms of verbs abound in its messages: *buy, go, bring, use, always have, take advantage of, decide, don't forget, remember, take, enjoy,* and they all mean the same thing: *obey.* Now with the tuning of the voices of the sirens, the message is becoming indirect, and maybe the imperative form will yield its place to a language in which the announcer becomes more vague. Then the message "I am the best" will gradually change to "We are beautiful," "We are good," "We love the world," "We love humanity," *"Don't stop buying our products."*

Is this reprehensible? Consumer society sells itself as the great provider. Finally, man has entered the

larder of an opulent and happy world. There is free-
dom to purchase, equality of prices, brotherhood in
consumption. It doesn't seem open for discussion
whether it is better to choose among five or ten qualities
and fragrances of soap or be condemned to the black
soap of the earth. That it is good to have at one's dis-
posal electric bulbs, refrigerators, ovens, furniture, innumerable things which individually we couldn't make.
How could one dare to raise his voice against demo-
cratic industry, which loses sleep just to offer humanity
so many necessary things, so many things which would
be inordinately expensive if they weren't mass produced?
Aren't the companies the bulwarks of democracy, the
antidotes to scarcity, the walls which protect us from
barbarism and misery? Aren't they also filling the world
with adorable creatures that remind us of our duty to
be beautiful, to be young, to be healthy and happy?

I believe humanity would do well to distrust and
suspect. There is a long history of powers who position
themselves above all criticism and feel authorized to do
as they choose by offering some benefit. Despite the
many benefits (and these we should also count) that
industry offers us, it cannot position its interests above
the primary interests of society. The truth is that the
only interest of capital is income, the accumulation of
excessive wealth which it reinvests without end. As long
as this goal is compatible with the well-being of its consumers, everything is almost fine — but it is clear that
when its ends come into conflict with that well-being of

society, it is not capital who warns us or corrects the
situation. The stories of the aerosol industry, the pesti-
cide industry, the detergent and plastic industries form
the most recent and alarming chapter of the Universal
History of Infamy. And we are all aware that the first
temptation of industry, when it finds itself under suspicion, is not to filter its toxic gases, nor to purify its
wastes, nor to modify its processes, nor to exclude harm-
ful ingredients, but to resort to the seductive voice of
the sirens to distract the public and reduce suspicions.
Thus, when a corporation launches a loud campaign
about some product which is non-polluting or ecologi-
cally benevolent, the operation is usually a smokescreen
to obscure their silence about the behavior of their other
products. Capital is extremely reluctant to change its
processes or risk its profitability for trivial humanitar-
ian considerations. And this is due to the basic reality
that capital is blind to everything except its basic activities of production, distribution, commerce, reinvest-
ment and accumulation. We cannot ask that the dragon,
in his hour of hunger, think of the feelings of the dam-
sel who is chained to the rocks. Thus vigilance must be
imposed. Meanwhile science pushes blindly forward in
its rush to know, without any notion of ethics. Technology pushes blindly forward in its task of dominating the
world, without the slightest notion of any ethics. Industry rushes blindly forward in its labor of transforming
the materials of the universe into consumer goods, without even asking itself what is necessary, what is useful,

what is superfluous, what is damaging, what things
make us more civilized and what things make us more
passive or even more barbarous. It only matters that
these things can be advertised and sold, to keep the
machines producing, the televisions announcing and
advertising, and the supermarkets selling, in a thought-
less, frenetic and wasteful carnival. As if now that dreams
are dead, all we have are our appetites. As though only
that which has been conceived and produced by human technology could be desirable and trustworthy.
And this is leading us to distrust even the agreeable
traditional system of reproduction, as we move toward
fabricating humanoids in genetic laboratories and even
in mechanical workshops. It's quite a spectacle, the
exquisite artifacts made from omnipresent non-biodegradable substances, the innumerable foolish and hid-
eous objects that one encounters in North American
malls, the infinite trinkets that all buy and none use,
the clothes that grow old in the closets of industrial
society without ever being worn, the stored meat that
rots, the machines that get thrown away upon their
first slight flaw, the cemeteries of debris that grow and
grow and soon will bury the utopia of Metropolis.

Obediently advertising announces all of it, applauds
all of it, and makes efficient use of the countless and
occasionally astonishing technical resources of commu-
nication. With its capacity to seduce and condition human behavior, it has continued to invade man's space,
to suggest or impose products and brands, to dictate

fashion, to create celebrities and to design styles and social conduct. Today, when not appearing in the press or on television is equivalent to not existing, this cult of image and success seems to be converting our real life into a second-class reality and the simulacrum of advertising, as well as the simulacrum of journalism, into the only respectable reality.

The messages no longer require arguments. The techniques of seduction only demand that they pleasantly affect the senses and produce the intense sensation in the public that their necessities will be satisfied. It was inevitable that on this path even the most serious and transcendental things would end up trivialized into mere images of seduction. There is no longer a place on the planet where politics doesn't turn to the advertising industry to help design and sell the image of its candidates. What should they promise? That which the opinion polls tell them is popular. Should they demonstrate character, or maybe familiarity and sympathy? It depends on who they have to compete with. An image is worth a thousand words, they say, which makes it more valuable to publish convincing photographs and dispense with words and commitments as much as possible.

It was on the basis of advertising, more than any other factor, that Adolf Hitler rose to power in Germany and that his vengeful nationalist discourse swelled among his people. This should be enough to awaken suspicion regarding this apparently neutral technique.

An instrument which serves equally well to impose perfume and tyranny, ought to demand great vigilance and awaken prudent suspicion. But humanity abdicates its important duties of control and resistance, and the planet is struggling with a plague of lying, vacillating, corrupt statesmen, who have idolized the media and who subject themselves to the whims of public opinion in making even the most important decisions. One couldn't find a publicist who thinks that selling a candidate is substantially different from selling a soft drink or selling a car. Everything is a question of the adequate image, of the necessary climate of trust, of the exceptional slogan whose function usually isn't to summarize a thought, but to be clearly identifiable and distinct from any other candidate's image.

It is this grotesque manipulation which we call democracy. Wouldn't it be crazy to choose a ship's captain based on his photograph, his smile, or what his supporters say about him? Nonetheless, we increasingly leave grave matters in the hands of the least qualified opportunists, since we no longer demand programs nor ideas nor commitments, but only seductive images and successful smiles.

Moreover, the worst evil that we can attribute to industrial society and its sirens is the contrast between the fantasy universe they sell us and the growing prostration of the multitudes who are unable to purchase it. Like all heavens, this one had to engender a hell as its correlate. Today's hells are the junkyards of industry and consumerism, where those who have nothing fight to survive; those that have neither beauty, health, nor youth, neither success nor fortune; for whom the dominant discourse of an opulent and happy society would be a sad joke if it were not the reason why each day they surrender more to the pressures of an obscenely inaccessible ideal.

It is easy to find them in the junkyards or on the merciless streets, in the ruinous suburbs of what they call the developed world, but more than anywhere else they grow in the monstrous cities of those regions called, with a science fiction slang, the Third World. It is understood that if success and even dignity today depend on the capacity to consume, then these beings will be viewed by the ruling ideology as mere human garbage.

The pleasant paradise seems enough in itself, and it is sustained by all those who, docile in the face of temptation, strive to situate themselves in the respectable zone of consumption. Cars, furniture, electric appliances, credit cards, prepaid insurance and annual vacations confer on those who obtain them, through self-denial, the comfortable condition of human beings, free of the atrocious suspicion of failure. For failure is the demon of the century, and it is only measured in terms of exclusion from the consumer paradise. We can be cruel, stingy, unfaithful, indifferent to human suffering, egotistical, avaricious, discourteous and ethically deplorable; nobody will find in these shortcomings the failure of your existence. But failing to ac-

quire, and to sustain the impatient avidity of capital-
ism, is equivalent to losing your place in the order of
the world. For those who throw themselves into this
confusing bustle of the defeated, there will be neither
piety nor solidarity, neither cordiality nor justice.

Those of us who are residents of the Third or pos-
terior world need not make even a minor mental effort
to understand the characteristics of the inferno of this
opulent society of consumerism, this glossy and radi-
ant industrial society; all we have to do is walk out onto
the street. The children of indigence pass with dirty
blankets draped over their shoulders. They come from
the garbage dumps, or they are on their way back to
them. We can imagine the apocalyptic landscapes where
they pass their lives: fetid horizons under the shadows
cast by vultures, mountains of refuse, the detritus of
civilization, the final fruit of optimism and human
progress converted into the kingdom of the last men.
Thus they pass on the periphery of our daily activities.
They come from misery, and they return toward it; in
passing by us they remind us, in an ironic gesture of
the gods of justice, of everything which advertising has
strained itself to make us ignore or forget: that illness
exists, that old age exists, that death exists, and that
the proud towers of our civilization are constructed with
cement which is corroded by insensitivity. Then we feel
that there — where there are no perfumes but instead
their broken flasks, where there is no fashion but tat-
tered refuse — there, among the indestructible plastics

and alongside foaming dirty streams, maybe the true world and the real future will be announced. It is then that we almost understand the pathetic desperation with which the new fascists, who will not even dare to show their faces, go out into the night to assassinate the homeless sleeping under bridges, to try in a mindless way, drunk on barbarous ineptitude, to erase the evidence of our present disorder — trying to convince themselves that the miserable are responsible for the misery. And it is then that we also understand that perhaps what the world needs is not more goods, more cars, more mansions, more progress, and more advertising, but instead a little bit of human generosity, a more vigilant review of the opulent future falsely promised by the phantoms, a little bit of honesty with our souls, and a little bit of prudence in the brief and dangerous time which has been granted to us.

the icy gaze

"IT IS DIFFICULT TO CONTINUE BEING EMPEROR IN FRONT OF A doctor," says Hadrian at the beginning of Yourcenar's novel, "...and even difficult to conserve the feeling of being human." Reading these words, I believed I could understand a little bit the secret fear which not only doctors but the whole realm of their labors have inspired in me. The tense silence of the waiting rooms, the desolate peace of the hospitals, the terrible miracle of the operating rooms. It is possible that the fear these spaces infuse is due to the lurking presence of patient and inexorable Death, who will have to show his face one day — but it is also possible that this fear is born from the institutions themselves.

In reality, few things so reduce man to defenselessness and impotence as the power of doctors. If a man offers us his help he is our equal, but if he goes on to take our pulse it feels like we are at his mercy. Virtually no field of human knowledge grants its owner as much power over other people as this ancient and prestigious profession we call medicine. Once it was restricted to magic and miracles; today it is a division of science, and it branches persistently into ever more sophisticated and onerous specialties. Through the centuries its practitioners were demigods like Empedocles, gods like Aesculapius, wise men like Celsus, extremely wise men like Paracelsus, demiurges, wizards, shamans, miracle-workers, and thaumaturgists. They had been given the most beautiful of virtues: the ability to cure, to snatch mortal flesh from the hands of death and return it unharmed to this marvel which is our world. They deserved all possible gratitude and all possible veneration. They also alternated the medicines of their science with the medicines of hope. They were subordinate to other mysteries; they didn't aspire to raise Maya's veil, to be owners of an unquestionable and absolute knowledge. They were sacred beings who performed a function sometimes rational, sometimes magical, in an enchanted world.

In that incredibly remote world — where faith moved mountains, where ingenuousness allowed for belief in miracles and frequently made them occur — these magical powers were the attributes of a few beings, but the truth is that the common people participated in a certain basic primordial knowledge. Tradition had bequeathed to humanity, generation after generation, many secrets and much wisdom to face this net of great wonders and small sorrows that we call life. Pains, fevers, spasms, pallors, fainting, wounds, dislocations,

lacerations, fractures, that rainbow of ailments which
ranges from blood-red to the green of fainting, passing
through dark purples and violets, was continually read
by the knowledge of tradition. They worked with the
powers of herbs and barks, of beneficial juices and sul-
furic waters; the all-embracing powers of lemon and
honey, of aromas and ointments, of lunar waters and
distillations of fruits and leaves; the techniques of punc-
tures and cupping glasses, of aromatic smoke and fast-
ing, of tonics and massages, the infinite resources of
memory, improvisation and hope.

Of course the Second and Fourth Horsemen of the
Apocalypse passed many times, harvesting human life
and plundering the nations terribly. Death was never
defeated, but I dare to think that usually the principal
dangers of the species were news and religions — princes
and priests rather than plagues and illnesses. Today we
can confirm that certain epidemics, like cholera, result
from poverty and social disorder rather than random
morbidity.

With an eternal mixture of herbs and tenderness,
innumerable generations cured many minor — and occasionally major — maladies. Today's natural doctors,
as well as those who prescribe placebos, would tell us
that the reason for this consists primarily in the fact
that the principal remedy to sickness of the body has
always been within the body, in its capacity to react
and resist — in the body, which is an expression of will,
as Schopenhauer thought — in the body, and in that

cloud of dreams which impregnates it that we call the soul. Many times the enchanters and surgeons concentrated on using their influence and power to reinforce these reserves of enthusiasm, this miraculous will to live which is the true nucleus of all existence. Changing the attitude of the body itself and its relationship to the illness could be the beginning of healing. This type of attitude, at once both illusory and practical, must have been the basis of many miracles.

But such wisdom seems to be the privilege of simplicity and ignorance, and we find ourselves in a world where reason has triumphed. With the gods dead or absent, man has remained alone, suspicious of all transcendent orders, disowning everything which is not evident, negating even the existence of his own spirit, and trusting only the powers of knowing, of reason, and of human labor. Modern positivism, excluding everything which is outside reason and its methods, everything which cannot be logically proven, has reduced man to the poor dimensions of materiality and evidence. It is the desanctified expression of a world made only from blind material, a cold mechanism governed by inflexible and impassive laws where there is no room for active forces as causes of reality — where there is no room for passion, or hope, or dreams, or faith, or beauty, and no shelter for the divine in the world.

Something like this had happened, very briefly, in the last days of the Roman Empire. Flaubert wrote that in those times, with the pagan gods dead and Christ not yet triumphant, man was alone in a world without transcendental meaning — such was Hadrian's century. Thus when Yourcenar writes about this emperor, she seems to be describing our times, since we too live in an age from which the gods are absent, and in which the very sense of the divine has been lost. For the same reason, Hadrian's doctors are neither priests nor auspex, neither magicians nor thaumaturgists. They aren't those wise men capable of seeing in a human being the complex fabric of functions and dreams — of languages and inventions of which these functions and dreams are constituted — but scientists who only see a sad amalgamation of lymph and blood. Before the gaze which has reduced reality to the functional and the evident, before the terrible gaze of positivism, "it is difficult to continue being emperor and even difficult to conserve the feeling of being human."

In our times almost no one has conserved this feeling. Beneath the cold, dispassionate, impartial gaze of science, we are only mortal flesh altered by illnesses or already trapped in inexorable conditions. It matters little if the doctor is more or less cordial, more or less compassionate. The mental universe to which he pertains is the universe of fatal atoms, and in that kingdom there is room for neither the magic of hope, nor the mountains of faith, nor even the disorder of miracles.

I remember Yuri Gagarin's surprising declaration that he had gone into outer space and proven that God wasn't there. The poor Marxist positivist wanted thus to dissolve forever the illusion of divinity, as though the spectacle of the starships was necessary, as though we didn't know that the priests of positivism and their followers had also been unable to observe the divine in the world. If we want to know how positivism defines man, we need look only at bacteriological examinations, hematic charts, glycemic curves, electrocardiograms — the words are almost as terrible as what they describe — and electroencephalograms. Now there is nothing left inside us but quantifiable material, measurable space, the abandoned fabric of our cells, the vertiginous abyss of our atoms — identical to the vertiginous abyss of the stars where the naïve and obedient cosmonaut couldn't see God.

We seem to conserve none of the sacred fire which sparkled in the words of Buddha or Christ, none of the powerful myths that were once our substance. A framework of calcium covered with tissues and liquids, a structure of processes and functions where all the inexplicable is silenced. We believed that the universe was a magical chorus of stars proclaiming the love that moves them, as Dante thought, but the wise men have come to tell us that it is no more than an abyss of solitude and vertigo, the infinite without sense or meaning whose silence terrified Pascal. We believed that the world was an orb of powers and gods, a tragic garden of beauty and song, but someone has come to tell us that there is no divinity in the forests nor sacredness in the waters. Every thing that advanced in beauty like Byron's night can be transformed into garbage and rubble. The stamp of the inscrutable gods has been erased from all things, and now they can only bear the symbols of industry, the greedy logos that have taken possession of even mystery in the world. We have repeated with Hamlet:

What a piece of work is a man! how noble in reason, how infinite in faculty! in form and moving how express and admirable! in action, how like an angel! in apprehension how like a god! the beauty of the world, the paragon of animals!

But the wise men have come to show us the finished and complete image of our being. What science has been able to see using its most potent rays is no more than that scheme of shadow and bones which our X-rays reveal.

But then where are dreams and love, generosity and hope, the soul full of gods and the flesh full of memories? Is none of this important? Does none of this exist? Does none of this count in the moments when we face the world, face solitude, and face the mystery of illness and the majesty of death?

The spirit of this age proceeds in a curious manner. In all fields man loses dominion of his world. He creates less and he decides less, while the news continues to spread that we have never been more perfect, more important, and more content. At the same time that they preach the sermon of supremacy, the gospel of comfort, the exaltation of the human as the ultimate end of all evolution and all progress, what we see is the progressive loss of space of every individual human being. Now the only trips are the prefabricated and conventional itineraries of tourism. Now nothing of our reality remains which does not become merchandise. Now we are not even the protagonists of our own lives. He who wants to know what happened yesterday does not look into his own memory, but consults television news and the newspapers. Above the anonymity, solitude, and undervaluation of millions and millions of singular beings, as mysterious and mortal as any, floats an artificial cloud of celebrities fabricated by industry, advertising, and journalism, to provide lavish anecdotes and to be sold as spectacles. And politicians and statesmen are also part of this chorus of successful faces which are endlessly sold to us; we must choose among them based on their profiles and their toothy grins.

We are beating a retreat from all orders of reality. Where the Renaissance left us the illusion of being universal men — interested in both the earth and the waters, in both air and fire, curious about the infinite diversity of creatures, forms and disciplines — now the severe crowd of specialists has arrived, and each one proceeds to expel us from his or her parcel. The refined modern world does not tolerate vain speculators on far-flung topics. He who wants to survive, compete in his profession, and make it profitable must continually narrow his field of vision and know more and more about progressively fewer things.

What we never imagined is that this curious process of the eviction of man from everything which previously gave meaning to his life — this process by which capital expelled us from all of the places which made up our kingdom so as to make us pay for each of them, for love, for friendship, for the world, for the stars, for the water and the air — would bring us to this alarming and extreme situation of being expelled from our own selves and from all knowledge about our own substance. Science declared illegitimate and groundless all the knowledge which tradition had left us about our own bodies. It confined this knowledge to the territory of superstition, and raised itself up as the sole proprietor of valid knowledge about health and illness, and life and death.

After it had completed this task, the increasing use of technology in diagnosis came next. Where previously basic knowledge of physiology was sufficient to identify a common dysfunction or disease, more sophisticated equipment and more refined procedures came to be necessary. Are the diagnoses really more precise? Possibly, but we can be sure that they are more costly. And who is not disposed to invest in certainty when it addresses the most important matter of health? Didn't Schopenhauer write that health is happiness? Everything then, should be subordinated to its achievement and conservation. Curiously, it seems to be of little importance that more than half of humanity is fatally excluded, due to poverty, from the enjoyment of these benefits which are proclaimed indispensable.

Additionally, there are now sensible doctors who affirm that this complex apparatus of tests, analysis, and technology cannot always replace the wisdom of a good doctor of the type who knows how to see the whole body as an organic unit, interdependent and sensitive, in which fear, enthusiasm and hope also operate. Now there are sensible individuals who suspect that it is not always the quest for more and better knowledge which drives these technical refinements, but the avidity of capital which has encountered another field of activity — an immense market — in the afflictions of the flesh. If health is the most precious, why should it be cheap? If one can pay tribute, and does it happily for the spirits of Hippocrates, why should he abstain?

Over this once venerable field also loom other sinister clouds. Nobody denies that health is now a product. Not only are the mechanisms of diagnosis expensive, but the pharmaceutical laboratories are vast industrial emporiums, capitalist companies as interested in gain as any others — companies with an interest in increasing and augmenting consumption. One could imagine Alka-Seltzer obtained a not insignificant doubling of their sales by putting not one but two effervescent tablets in the same glass of water in all their commercials. And we also should not forget that the virtuous pharmaceutical industries are often owned by larger companies which produce insecticides and other chemical calamities. The good angels have unexpected horns of gold. Ancient alchemy, too, knew how to distill its poisons. I remember that Ernesto Cardenal, in one of those poems of his which derive from the masterful work of Ezra Pound, says that there are companies that today present themselves as the jealous guardians of the salvation of humanity, when in other moments they have been less gentle — like a certain producer of condoms who also fabricated another synthetic substance: napalm.

The most important factor is that now we don't know very well who are the friends of the human race. Industry, which is at times so generous with pleasant and useful products, is completely heartless in the moment of decision-making. It does good and evil with the same amazing intensity, because the only thing which governs it is the mysterious haste of capital which, like cancer, knows only how to grow and proliferate at the expense of the organism which nourishes it.

Now ignorant and unconscious of our own bodies, now at the mercy of experts and industry, the forces of alienation did not want to detain themselves with these few achievements. What can happen when man finds himself defenseless in the hands of knowledge and technology — when the possibility of survival becomes converted, thanks to progress, into something so onerous that it ends up being unthinkable? In this instance the serpent of modernity seems to have bitten its own tail;

it seems to have created a vicious circle of necessity and impotence within a disconcerted humanity, heir to the ancient curse of pain and death. In the hour of illness nobody is the owner of knowledge, but the expense of the knowledge has made it inaccessible. Thus we arrive at the perfection of the system, in which every human being pays from the beginning and forever for the health which he wants to enjoy in this world. All of us, ill or healthy, must pay a monthly tribute to the universal coffers of knowledge which one day will snatch us from the greedy gullet of death — saving us at the same time from financial ruin, now that the more expensive and specialized doctors, the more technical and exhaustive diagnoses, the more aseptic and wondrous operating theaters, the more comfortable and onerous hospitals, and the unaffordable medicines, would cost us the eyes from our face or a whole life mortgaged to creditors.

It also becomes important that man pay continuous attention to his fragility and vulnerability. It is good that unexpected revelations about possible sicknesses should lie in ambush in the pages of the magazines. Illness is always suspended like the famous sword over the necks of the mortals, so that they learn to depend on the card from their health insurance company as they previously depended on divine mercy.

But even if illness must be a continuous and insidious threat, it certainly need never arrive — not because industry especially appreciates the health of men, but because continuous health is a precondition of productivity. Thus illness is abominable only because it paralyzes the payroll. Nobody should get ill now that their work is waiting for them. It is even offensive for an employee to get sick during workdays, since he has two long weeks of vacation to use for such purposes. This zeal to impede the arrival of illness is manifested in those commercials which always begin by saying, "Upon the first symptom of cold or flu, take this or that...." Illness is continually rejected or postponed, and set up as the supreme expression of the abnormal and the undesirable.

But maybe there are a few things which could be said in favor of illness. Not only that it is more normal than this sick society claims — not only that denying it, smothering it and fleeing from it are not the best way of dealing with it — but that it forms part of the mysterious cycle of life, and it offers to teach us things we can't learn from good health. For one thing, if the time of good health is time for the world, the time of illness could be the time for the individual, for introspection, for spiritual absorption, for the journey through the mysteries of the body and through its relation with the natural universe. The custom doctors have of keeping secret the illnesses which they are diagnosing and curing, and of prescribing substances which we must consume in a silence of complicit and submissive ignorance, makes us live far from our bodies and from some of their most alarming manifestations.

Why does modern civilization want us to live with

our backs to our most profound certainties? Why does
the knowledge of death have no place in the order of
our world? Why is illness managed in this double condition of constant danger and constant exile, as a threatening state which must never arrive and against which
the army of medicine and its industry stands constant
guard? One of the answers is that in some way the truth
could set us free. The certainty of death is so difficult to
bear that for more than two thousand years we pre-
ferred dreaming of the risk of an eternity of suffering to
admitting the possibility of death. The vertiginous and
unsustained idea of an eternal life, in monotonous choruses which never end or in equally enduring stinking
furnaces, seemed more pleasant and merciful.

But in our melancholy age of triviality and garbage, of positivism and health by quotas, of material
without spirit and the rapid race toward the most ugly;
in this age the wise men have been capable of demon-
strating that without deteriorating the gifts of life, its
splendor and its ineffable miracles, death can also be a
blessing. Death, with its uncertainties and its mytholo-
gies, with its thick layers of shadow and its abysses,
with its promise of indifference and oblivion, with its
rivers that erase memory and its unpredictable deriva-
tion of the eternal from the temporal; with its dense,
solitary, inevitable, and almost superhuman mystery.
But accepting that we are moving toward this irrevers-
ible destiny imposes happiness as a condition of life.
Nobody who serenely accepts death as a certainty can

permit his life to be made a servile donation to the coffers of greed, a trivial figure in the choruses of a cruel and stupid world. The certainty of death, with the tragic aura that it drapes over every minute of our lives, makes the hasty spectacle of the world brilliant and valuable. It fills life with so much supernatural horror toward cruelty and its crimes, with so much nobility toward the beautiful and the generous elements of human existence. It imposes so much respectful silence where there was so much presumptuous knowledge. It diminishes our arrogance so much, and magnifies our happiness so much, that we would never let ourselves live as slaves to the farces of the world. We could not continue to be indifferent witnesses to the suffering of living beings, and frenetic purchasers of illustrious garbage or stunned consumers of colorless spectacles. This difficult truth — the certitude of pain, of decrepitude and termination — could make us more valiant and more free. It could allow us to participate in the celebration of the world without the clumsy pride of those who believe themselves eternal, but with the lucid liberation of those who know that all is promised to nothingness.

Only thus can health and illness retrieve the transcendental sense of the dignity of life and the majesty of death. Thus the myths, the music, the symbols, inexplicable nature, the miracle of the arts and the power of the elements, the tapestry of dreams and the abyss of memory, the soul full of gods and the flesh full of memory, make us raise our voice against the poverty of a world which wanted to simplify us into mere evident material and measurable processes. We will remember that capital, the sciences, and the technologies which serve them have transformed human life into a tributary of industry, an element which must function well for strictly economic reasons. We will remember that in these times, when man was near death he was converted into a disposable terminal organism, useless for capital and without sense for science, exactly at that point where man, alive and sacred until the ultimate instant, is maybe more lucid and more full of exciting visions. We will understand that the life we were promised is different and the death we were promised is different, and even if these forms of human dignity and human nobility are never realized, nothing, not even the icy gaze of the basilisk, can rob us of our hope.

the shipwreck of metropolis

MANY RECENT MOVIES, ESPECIALLY NORTH AMERICAN FILMS, play the strangely suggestive game of weaving variations on the theme of the decline and fall of the great cities of our age. One of them, more notable for its theme than for its artistic achievements, shows a ruined New York, abandoned to the ruffians and rats. In another film I remember the severed head of the Statue of Liberty halfway submerged in the rubble. *Metropolis*, *Blade Runner*, *Brazil* are examples of a somber glance at our expectations for cities. But more and more we have the sensation that these phantasmagorias of the cinema or of literature are no idle caprices, but presentiments, and at times even mirrors, of reality.

In the violent streets of the Bronx, in the melancholy buildings of the Parisian *Banlieu*, in the circular highways which ring Florence, in the *comunas* of Medellin, or in the tall buildings of central São Paolo, one can sense that cities are no longer the crowns of civilization. They are swelling and inhuman labyrinths where anguish and tedium alternate, where perhaps even more terrible creatures are gestating.

Nonetheless, the city was once our pride, and one of our great dreams. It seems to have been traced in the hearts of man since long before the first pyramids. Αντροποσ φυσει πολιτικον ξωον, Aristotle wrote, and this can only mean that man is by nature an urban creature, an inhabitant of the *polis*. Forget about Rousseau's theory that humans are imaginable in the breast of a happy natural world, uncontaminated by culture. Everything has come to demonstrate that culture is the natural ambit of man and that outside of culture we are especially defenseless creatures, alarmingly lacking in instincts.

We may have lived for centuries in the meadows of Arcadia, on ranches, or in cabins in the forests, but history was centered in and governed by the cities. In these tropics, almost all of us are children and grandchildren of farmers — of hardworking and simple beings who endured their whole lives among mountains and rivers, of men for whom savage countryside was the whole universe — but from childhood we have known that antiquity was ruled by vast cities. Before our grandfathers trimmed the forests from the mountains of America, our ancestors had lived in Madrid or in Seville, in the beautiful cities of Anahuac or behind stone walls on severe Andean summits. Before that they had traveled from Paris and Santiago and Aix-la-Chapelle and Mainz and Rome; they had besieged Istanbul, and they had seen the blue mosques of Baghdad. Before these modernities, when Allah had not yet flowered on the dry lips of the prophet, Rome had reigned beneath the eternal stars and had razed Carthage. Rome had paved the roads, uniting London with the capital of Byzantium and Italy with the cities of Cappadocia and Bythinia. And all of that was no more than an echo of the cities Alexander had founded on his incredible voyage, the Alexandrias and Bucephaluses he had erected to his gods. Or the surprising cities he encountered and humbled, like Thebes and Tyre; or those that he encountered and fell in love with, like Susa; or those that he encountered and cast into the sky as smoke, like Persepolis. And even before this there were Memphis and Babylonia, and that Ur which first read the stars; the sky sustained by the caryatids of Athens, harsh winds blowing over the high walls of Troy, and the muddy confines of Nineveh.

Great cities are as old as the wheel and the power over fire. Princes ruled, actors performed, and bureaucracies flourished in them. Generals made war, priests conspired, eunuchs intrigued, and slaves were humiliated in them. The city was an ideal projection of man: his provisions in the market, his health in the gymnasiums, his pain in the hospitals, his power in the palaces, his eloquence in the public squares, his spirit in the theaters, his veneration in the temples, his conclusion in the cemeteries, his equilibrium in the courts, his insanity in the sanatoriums, his rebellion in the jails, his supremacy on the thrones.

The distribution of the cities revealed the type of social order which each group had attained. Their architecture revealed the secrets of their spirit: curious about nature, as in the pagan cities, or fearful of it, as in the Christian cities; constructed with an architecture to intimidate, like the Palace of Versailles, or to seduce, like the Palace of the Alhambra. The urban world was full of possible games and possible dreams. And while confidence in the destiny of the species still endured, cities were mechanisms of beauty, monuments to the knowledge of man, to his talent, to his pride — meditated works of art.

Some will say that since the most distant times ugliness, dirtiness, garbage, poverty, the rubble of wars and injustices, and pockets of plague and pestilence have existed. This cannot be denied — but before the eighteenth century the world was wide and diverse; it pertained more to every individual, and even the slaves had a certain margin of singularity. Caught by pirates in the waters of the Mediterranean and sold as a slave in Crete, Diogenes the Cynic not only convinced the auctioneer to let him hawk himself, but also passed the whole afternoon quizzing passersby as to who was sufficiently sensitive to become his owner. It is now well known that he found a buyer.

The city was the great dream of the species, and the distinct utopias which human dissatisfaction envisioned were woven into fantastic cities governed by philosophers or angels, ordered according to the algebra of reason or the imperatives of the divine. The city of God, the city of the Philosopher-King, the Spartan city of the warrior, the fabulous cities of Marco Polo, the fantastic Babylon of Voltaire, and the ideal Rome of Piranesi: the city sprang from reality to fantasy; there was not a sage who did not dream of a perfect city. And each was subject to an evident or tacit divinity: an Athens consecrated to knowledge; a Rome dedicated to Jupiter, and thus to power and the law; a Lutecia dedicated to Venus, and thus to pleasure and love; a Florence consecrated to the arts; a Sybaris devoted to the art of living; a Sodom dedicated to voluptuousness; a Baghdad and an Alexandria consecrated to learning, a Jaujas to abundance and a Capuas to pleasure, and a buried Atlantis of golden centuries.

But it seems that from a certain moment forward, the cities of the imagination began to darken — not only to resemble the worst of the real cities, but to magnify their worst traits dramatically. The vision of poverty suggested infinite neighborhoods of unemployment and indifference. The rise of the machine created immense manufacturing districts overwhelmed by smog and soot. The boom in production created endless businesses. In this disappearance of the splendid fantasies was encoded humanity's loss of faith in the possibilities of the city, as well as the death or flight of the divinities that were its center and its spirit.

Abruptly we find ourselves hurled into what today

is called the real city. It is found in the poems of Baudelaire, a swarming metropolis tyrannized by work and tedium where the spirit can find refuge only in the artificial paradises of absinthe and opium. It is found in the novels of Dickens, where mistreated and lonely human beings survive the adversity of a world at once populous and vacant. It is found in the novels of Balzac, where bourgeois society eats, works and plays stripped of all idealism, moved only by the force of profit. It is found in Dostoyevsky and in Henry James, and it advances, darkening, toward the pitiless urban mechanisms in which man is a foreigner and is always lost: the city of the stories and novels of Franz Kafka.

With the arrival of our own century, the city appeared to have reached its limit. On June sixteenth, 1904, two almost imaginary beings, a young poet named Stephen Dedalus and a fifty-year-old businessman called Leopold Bloom, perused for the last time the ideal city of philosophers and dreamers, and traveled for the first time the debilitating labyrinth of the prosaic city; stripped of sanctity, the cold godless universe of the modern city; crowds and trolleys, innumerable unknown destinations, simultaneous and parallel; the physical space a badly combined mixture of buildings and businesses over a substrate of tunnels and tubing — the obscure entrails of the city which discharge their dark detritus to the blind immensity of the oceans. In that moment, the process which calls itself modernism was consummated. Since then, the European soul, and the souls of its many children all over the planet, have not been able to escape from that world which Joyce captured with splendid and almost superhuman clarity. Since then, almost all the cities of Western literature correspond to that detailed map of the spiritual Dublin of 1904: the phantasmagoric London of Chesterton, the meticulous and lavish world of Proust, the Manhattan of John Dos Passos, and the almost intolerable Berlin of Alfred Doblin.

Almost all the cities dreamed up by science fiction also correspond to this realm — from the absolute cities of J.G. Ballard to the stellar cities of Frederick Pohl, and from the mysterious neighborhoods of Bradbury to Philip K. Dick's city which Ridley Scott made shockingly visible to us.

Under these clouds of light and these symbols of the imagination, the real cities have grown. And they differ very little from their illustrious imaginary replicas. Mexico City is becoming the infinite city, and London and Los Angeles extend into the dark like phosphorescent stains. The incredibly tall towers of Manhattan, Chicago and São Paolo invade the sky. Lagos and Buenos Aires expand around the mouths of their enormous rivers. The miserable neighborhoods, full of incertitude and violence, disturb the daily life of Rio de Janeiro and Bogotà. And nowhere do the troubles of the city seem to be diminishing, now that the city is stripped of its magical aura, now that it has been converted into a chaos of violence and noise.

It is true that many European cities and a few American cities still conserve a certain equilibrium which is the fruit of centuries of slow growth, foresight, discipline, a pedagogy of cohabitation, and an emphasis on civil ethics. It is true that in Paris and Boston, drivers do not aggressively hurl themselves at pedestrians. It is true that in many cities there is an elementary respect for the norms of coexistence in a thrown-together world. On the other hand, it is true that the confused Latin American cities demonstrate all of the disadvantages of urban life and none of its secular virtues. It is true that the inhabitants of Vienna and Madrid survive in better conditions than those entrapped inhabitants of the cities of Latin America. But the reason is that Mexico City, Buenos Aires, São Paolo, Caracas and Bogotà have grown to their current immeasurable proportions in little more than a half century. They have seen their populations multiply by ten or twenty times during this period, and their little colonial streets are not always able to adapt to the rapid and noisy machines which civilization has brought. They have been the first pathetic victims of this unexpected and urgent gift which the sages call progress and with which so few seem dissatisfied in the ruling capitals of the world.

But now there is so much belief in the material that no space remains for the spiritual; now there is so much information that there is scarcely room for understanding, and nonetheless so much understanding that no

space remains for wisdom. With so much haste, we
forget where we are going; with so much work, we forget that we work to live better; with so much consumption, we forget that it was important to be something
and to be someone; with so much passivity and so
many spectacles, we forget that it was the capacity to
create which made us human.

The last shall be first. These nations who were the
last to receive the legacy and the imperative of Western
civilization, will never obtain the abundance which Europe — or a European elite — enjoyed in the eighteenth
century. But now they are the first to suffer the disor-
ders and evils which the very idea of the city carried
hidden in its breast, and the evils with which history
has enriched itself.

What has made our cities grow in such a monstrous
way? General demographic growth is such that there
are almost as many human beings present today as
have lived since the beginning of history. One could say
that the number of the living and the number of the
dead from all the ages have reached equilibrium; they
form an astonishing equation which will not fail to be
highly stimulating for those who hunt the symbols and
augurs of modernity.

But humanity could still be very easily distributed
across the faces of the continents, cultivating the earth
in a reasonable way, being cautious not to plunder or
pillage the sacred universe which is the very condition
of our existence. The species could be organized in

semi-rural communities, well-educated, diligent, worshippers of ethics and aesthetics, respectful of nature, vigorous, emotionally healthy, free of prejudices, and comfortable with austerity. The greatest imaginable cultural diversity could bloom, and we could even take advantage of science and technology, and the planet would not even feel that it had humans living on it.

But everything has fallen into the hands of certain forces that have no interest in the conservation of the planet, that cannot be moved by the spectacular deterioration of human and natural life, and that can feel neither the sacred nor the divine in the world, for the sad and powerful reason that they aren't even able to feel: They are the immense corporations that govern everything today. They are heirs to the arrogance of the warriors, the haughtiness of the priests, and the egoism of the monarchs. They have only one objective: to convert the world and, if possible, the universe into one immense market. And human beings — including their own alienated administrators — they would change into dispossessed producers, who are not owners even of their own hands or their own hours, and into passive yet voracious consumers.

These active and ungovernable forces which produce and accumulate require a humanity which is concentrated and available, over which they can exercise their influence and to whom they can supply goods and services. While power was in the hands of the warriors, the kings, or the pontiffs, humanity could be scattered, dispersed in nations or tribes that were hostile to one another. But as the owners continue to unify themselves over all of the planet, the subjects are being unified as well. Diversity becomes an obstacle, and cities are erected as symbols which offer the masses the lure of happiness, comfort, and a prosperous and secure life. And thus the cities, in their ancient communal, intellectual and artistic sense, are disappearing both in reality and in the imagination. They are being replaced by cities of supermarkets and automobiles, of massive spectacles, of newspapers and television, of prepaid insurance, incessant banks, and credit cards.

Where there is abundance and the schemes of democracy function, this model could possibly work sometimes. A humanity stripped of all initiative will base its existence on the need to integrate into the mass rituals of work and consumption. They will obediently pay their fees; they will trade their cars in every year, and they will make their house payments indefinitely. They will enjoy the benefits of a medical insurance that unceasingly saves them from illnesses which are more costly every day; they will work all day in the office or the factory, and they will prepare or cook less and less of the food they eat. They will start each morning with the newspaper which exempts them from being protagonists of their own lives, and they will sit every night before the television which fills hours that otherwise would be dangerously vacant. They will watch television in all of their free time, or else they will go out to

shop compulsively in the endless stores, taking advantage of the sales that produce the sensation of getting a
good deal on products that they don't need at all. They
will go on vacation to repeat a ritual that now teaches
nothing and transforms no one, and these things they
will call, with more or less enthusiasm, *their happiness.*

But the same scheme projected over the other societies of the planet will produce different effects. The
cities of the so-called Third World also radiate their
dreams of happiness. They offer the possibility of work,
security, and prosperity to immigrants harassed by rob-
bery, by rural violence, and by poverty. In the city is
progress — factories, supermarkets, department stores
and cash machines, all-night clinics, celebrities, cin-
emas, the great spectacles — in short, real life.

Who wants to remain in the poverty of the small
farm? In its dark and abandoned nights where pain is
all-powerful, where insecurity is complete, where nature is, as Hegel thought, endlessly repetitive and te-
dious? The city is action, speed, animation, compan-
ionship; the city is happy, modern, full of seductions,
fashions, and adventures. On its corners could await
wealth, love, surprises — the sudden possibility of a
new life. The city is so powerful, it flings its tempting
message, drunk with promises, using all the tempting
languages of advertising. We should be surprised that
any of the poor remain in their fields and villages.

But evidently the city can't fulfill those beautiful

promises. It cannot find employment for all the people who arrive; it cannot offer them an agreeable house in a placid neighborhood. The surprises which await the dazzled travelers on the corners are different from what they expected. Instead, the miserable slums grow without end, and danger multiplies on the streets — because the legitimate obligation of those who lack everything and have no protection from society is to survive like the wolf on the frozen steppe. Dissatisfaction grows due to the great amount desired and the little obtained, when reality doesn't allow access to the many things which the television set proclaims to be indispensable goods and obligatory happinesses.

The crowd turns spiteful or at least bitter. We are in the heart of the promised land, and we have never been further from paradise. Every day brings disillusionment, but the promises continue flashing intact — only now there is neither will to oppose them nor arguments to evade them. Even though reality demonstrates time and again that the dream is impossible, the promise of the city is irrefutable, inevitable. Just as in a game, even though we have lost everything, the next round always promises triumph, which in all justice must arrive and will compensate all our efforts and all our suffering.

The mysterious power of this formidable illusion might have its source in more profound regions. We are accustomed to thinking of the problems of the world as isolated, unconnected and substantive, although everything allows us to suspect that they form part of an organic whole. The enormous city, the concentration of human beings and of the creatures whom they have tied to their destiny, also entails separation from nature — constructing a perfectly controlled orb where the margin of chance and risk can be computed at zero. I would say that the absolute city is born of the idea that man doesn't belong to the natural order, of the illusion that man is superior, and of the feeling that nature is evil or dangerous. The idea of superiority is the easiest of human errors, and it is perfectly understandable that for millennia we have made it our pride and our certainty. Gradually we made the gods human, so that there would be no doubt that the universe had been created by an authority of whom we are the image and likeness. This conferred on us certain divine privileges which the rest of nature did not share. Everything had to be subordinate to us: the Nile of time must pay tribute to us from its mud and its treasures. And the human city would be the visible crown of the universe, the throne of power and wisdom of which we would be the representatives and administrators.

That period was onerous for the world. In our condition as priests and spokesmen of despotic divinities, we could cause serious damage, and at times the only thing which protected the natural world was the admission that she also possessed divine attributes. But the triumph of Christianity definitively deprived nature of its sacredness. For the Greeks, there were divinities in the water, in the air, in the accumulation of the clouds, in the passing of time, in the blooming of the irises, in illness, and in death. For Christianity, divinity could only be manifested through the human, and the enemies of man were the Devil, the World and the Flesh — three powers that the pagans had exalted in the forms of Dionysus, Zeus and Aphrodite.

But what could be expected from that view of nature? If the Old Testament was repulsed by nature, we can understand the walls that it erected against her. Almost every mention of nature in the holy book is weighted down with a moral judgment: there is the tree of knowledge, the serpent is the devil, the apple is sin, God speaks in the burning bush, the rain is the flood of divine punishment, the rainbow is the text of reconciliation. Frogs, crabs, river water, and night's darkness are converted into the plagues which afflict Egypt. And when platonic spirituality is added to form Imperial Christianity, it is clear that nature remained excluded and converted into something terrible and undesirable.

At the end of the Middle Ages, a man as universal and lucid as Dante was able to use as a contrast to the image of the city — the symbol of culture and moral order — a dark jungle representing horror and chaos.

I would say that everything in Christianity, with the exception of the inexplicable and inspired figure of St. Francis of Assisi, was hostile to nature. It served as the foundation for a culture of exclusion and an arrogant anthropocentrism in which there was nonetheless no room for the most primitive and maybe the most essential forces of man.

There is a moving episode in Shakespeare's *Anthony and Cleopatra* which can illuminate the drama of the modern city for us. It is night in the Roman encampment on the eve of the definitive battle. The army sleeps. In front of the general's tent, two sentries stand guard. The arms piled in front of the tents glitter in the torchlight, which deepens into a silence full of omens. Suddenly a great murmur rises from the darkness. It is a music of oboes under the ground; as if a great entourage had begun marching, the uproar fills the air, but everything remains immobile and unchanged. At first only the two sentries hear it, then all of the soldiers. One asks another what this uproar is, what it could mean. The other responds, "It is the god Hercules who loved Anthony and now is abandoning him."

Although Swedenborg claimed he knew it, nobody has been able to define the exact year when the divine sense abandoned our world. The only certainty is that all of us were born into a world already stripped of its holiness. And curiously, this world thus impoverished didn't act more helpless, but instead more arrogant. The city was never so proud and imposing as when it stood divested of gods. Everything lacked meaning, but it was also freed from limits. Man was alone and was owner of the world, absolute master of the mountains and the jungles, of the depths of the sea and outer space.

It had never been so obvious that the Promethean powers had passed into our hands, that material was obedient to the dreams of reason. Now there were no restrictions; nothing detained progress; all the world would revere the law of man, and very soon the text of human supremacy would be heard in the high crevices.

Two centuries have passed since the French revolutionaries installed the cult of reason, soon after the promulgation of the Universal Declaration of the Rights of Man. Two centuries of solitude and supremacy have passed, and today we can see the result. All of the ancient and untouched universe begins to show the wounds that our blindness has inflicted, some of them possibly incurable. The indiscriminate looting of nature, viewed as a bank of resources, confronts us with the danger of the disappearance of forests and jungles, and with them the planetary air. Industrial waste and toxic vapors have perforated the ozone layer. The frenzy of output no longer permits the slow maturation of beings and trades; humanity is beginning to live a life like those experienced by birds and fish living in nurseries where they are submitted to a pressure to grow, so that they will develop at the rhythm dictated by capital. Projecting uniform spectacles for all humanity, modernity unifies and confuses the sexes, the generations, the cultures, in one indifferent amalgamation lacking colors or sense.

We had been taught that every human being was unique and precious before the powers of the unknown. Now only the quantifiable remains, and we are all the same: insignificant beings made of mortal material, who needn't create anything, who don't embody any singular truth, who only have to produce and consume according to the unappealable dictates of industry and of their servile assistants, science and advertising.

For an admirable paradox, the triumph of man, having become conceited in his cosmic solitude, seems too much like the defeat of man. Now it threatens to be also the defeat of all life, of the sublime adventure which could be called universal history.

And the cities — which were once our pride, and one of our great dreams, the crowns of civilization, the kingdom of friendship and the imagination — have become the stage where a humanity stripped of feeling and obligations, blind to the luck of their mysterious planet, present without knowing it the drama of their decline, the Shipwreck of Metropolis. They pathetically ignore the question of what will be the next episode in this threatening play, and whether this may not be the last.

Maybe they will fulfill the predictions of the prophets of science fiction. Maybe the atomic bombs will target a humanity delicately stacked in immense urban colonies; or the demographic bomb will convert humans into crazy termites that exterminate themselves; or the rivers of cars and indiscriminate industry and nightmarish indestructible plastics and unmanageable garbage will convert the cities into inhospitable kingdoms of neurosis, speed and disorder. Or maybe one day a humanity exasperated with itself, with its vehicular congestion, with its industrial frenzy, fed up with advertising, destroyed by fear, deaf from clatter, will remember that the immense countryside still exists, and will again embark on the path of a sensible and calm life. Or maybe a massive desertion of the human termite mounds will bring terror to the countryside as at times it has been brought to the city. None of these alternatives is more likely than the others.

I believe that only the rediscovery of the sacred sense of the world, only the return — unpredictable in its expression, its ethics and its aesthetics — of the divine, will permit humanity to recuperate its discreet and sublime place in the order of the universe. Only thus will we be able to see the reconciliation of man with nature, the passage from a time of domination to a time of alliance, and this will in turn permit the idea of the city — order, beauty and spirit — to recuperate the humble and sacred sense that it had before it converted itself into a nightmare.

latin america's responsibilities

WITH HIS CLASSIC HUMOR CONSTRUCTED OF LUCIDITIES and paradoxes, Jorge Luis Borges claimed that maybe we were the only Europeans, those of us who live in Latin America. From our distant position across the Atlantic Ocean, we see Europe as a totality of which we feel ourselves to be heirs, while nobody in Europe feels European, but barely Spanish or French, Swedish or German. We could look more closely and see how few feel themselves even to be Spanish, but instead Catalan, Basque or Gallego. The Serbs don't feel themselves to be simply a different people than the Croats, but from an entirely different planet. Even in Italy, a nation we often forget is composed of many formerly independent states, dialects abound; and of course being Irish obviously is not being English. Our America has persisted in the non-dialect use of the Castilian language, contributed by one of the many elements of our complex racial and cultural mixture. It has been conserved in such a manner that a man from Cuernavaca or Tegucigalpa can debate in a coffeeshop with a citizen of Colon, Cali or Valparaiso, and he will have only slight problems debating with a Spaniard — whose defect is a lack of universality, not in information, but in attitude.

The truth is that we are Europeans, but fortunately we are much more than Europeans. I say *fortunately* because — even forgetting the deluge of blood that our peninsular grandparents precipitated here, or considering it a normal example of the criminal stupidities of the human condition (Rome did no better with Carthage, nor the Aztecs with their neighbors, nor Japan with China) — there are other elements in the complex legacy of Europe which it would be wise to deplore and overcome. One of these qualities is the traditional notion of the superiority of all that is European.

Considering the order that Europe has constructed and diffused over the planet — that order which North American society has taken toward its natural conclusion — I would say that all of the legendary virtues of Europe are today under suspicion. From its intelligence have sprung the rationalisms. From its discipline have sprung totalitarianisms. From its patriotisms, the day before yesterday we saw the great Roman empire, yesterday we experienced Nazi barbarism, and today we are witnessing Serbian and Croatian brutalities. Due to its work ethic, we are drowning in a wasteful industrial warehouse. From its knowledge, we acquired the nuclear arsenals. From its faith sprang the Thirty Years' War and the Holy Inquisition. From its capacity for foresight and planning arise a threatening cloud of police states, of manipulative corporations, of genetic warehouses, of unmanageable refuse, and of defenseless humanity, which today are blossoming all over our planet.

What an injustice to the arts of Europe, to the philosophies of Europe, to the rich European imagination! What a blasphemy it is against Plato, against universal Leonardo, against harmonious Palladium, against the sublime genius of Mozart, against Kant and Nietzsche, to confirm that the most conspicuous and glorious cultural tradition of the planet is under suspicion. What would the world be, they will ask, without all the wonderful gifts of European culture — without Greek philosophy, without Christianity, without the songs of the troubadours, without the Divine Comedy; without Romeo's sighs, Ludwig van Beethoven's penultimate sonata for cello and piano, and Rembrandt's *Philosopher in Meditation*; without Brahms's violins, the Cathedral of Cologne, and Louis Pasteur; without the superhuman musical labyrinths of James Joyce? I have made this list in obedience to a few of the innumerable European products which, as Borges would say, "speak veneration to my heart." I hasten to add that I sincerely believe the world would be poorer, more desperate and sadder without them. But I also hasten to add that this cultural excellence is not exclusively European. The Eurocentrism of Western civilization has brought us to a situation where we appreciate, never sufficiently, but almost exclusively the creations of that region of the world, and it has subdued us in an astonished servitude. Europe is grand and beautiful and talented, but no more so than the rest of the world. Our servitude is not due to a hypertropic European creativity mutely accompanied by a surrounding planetary sterility, but to other reasons — which are worth examining if we want to save the world, and with it the exquisite roses of glass, of stone and of music engendered by our venerable ancestors in Europe.

One of the greatest virtues of the twentieth century has been to teach us to look at the Other with respect. Nationalist barbarisms are always characterized by a pride in the domestic idols and by a simultaneous blindness before foreign virtues. In the end, only one's own and the similar have always seemed perfect and beautiful. This is strange, because given the human constitution, it would seem that we always thrive on the external and the different. But Europe lived centuries upon centuries facing Africa, before Picasso arrived to discover that there was beauty in the ritual masks of those peoples who tend herds, cultivate and hunt further south, away beyond the Mediterranean. The reason why the *Demoiselles d'Avignon* have fascinated our age is that in painting those women, the artist knew how to fuse the dexterity of the Western tradition with the mysteries of that African universe which had been there in front of the Europeans forever, but which they had not been able to discover because they were too busy trading to it and dominating it. What can you think of a culture which enters into mysterious spheres, full of dark sublimity, like the plains of Africa — and instead of feeling drawn in and intoxicated by curiosity and veneration, dedicates itself to hunting the warriors, oppressing the maidens in chains and converting the priests into beasts of burden? One part of the millenarian history of Europe remains to be written, and our historians will not be the ones to write it. I dare to think that in that history Aimé Boupland will be more important than Napoleon Bonaparte, and the Baron Alexander von Humboldt more important than the ineffable professor George Frederick William Hegel, leading advocate of European hegemony and idolizer of progress.

This hegemony is especially familiar to the people of Latin America. Thus we learned that here there might be songs and rhythms, amusing ditties and curious sonorous inventions — but that real music, great music, is that controlled tempest which the symphony orchestras, the chamber orchestras and their masterful soloists effuse in funereal uniforms. And who could negate their greatness? But in what frame could one cultural tradition, no matter how attractive and fragrant it may be, occupy a station as the only language and the only path on such a vast and rich planet as this one? Don't all of these tacit and express impositions resemble the abusive pretension of the Roman church to be the only refuge for the soul, the secure ship outside of which there is no salvation? This tribal vice of excluding or judging all that is different is a very hu-

man characteristic, but no one has brought it to frui-
tion as effectively as the Europeans. Based on it, there
were Medic and Punic Wars, Octavian and Byzantine
Wars, Carolingian and Norman Wars. On these feelings
were based campaigns against Albigenses and Dollinists;
because of it so many children of the crusades were
turned into orphans, and later left their own children
orphaned. There were wars of blacks and whites, of
Guelphs and Ghibellines, of the forces of the empire
against the forces of the Papacy. For this vice Dante lost
his house, Cervantes his hand, Quevedo his tranquil-
ity, Rimbaud his leg, and poor Europe her best men in
1914. But a glance halfway free of superstition could
confirm that the cultural richness of the planet is ex-
traordinary, and that it is necessary — in reality a matter
of life and death — that those infinite traditions find a
way to cohabit and even reciprocally enrich one another without blood and idols establishing their exclu-
sions and hierarchies. Thus it is indispensable that we
admit that in affairs of the arts, of thinking, of sensibilities and of creation without commercial interest, there
is no progress, neither hierarchies nor possible suprema-
cies. The endless genius of Shakespeare does not surpass Basho nor the *Thousand and One Nights*. The
hand of Dürer is the same hand as that of the visitors to
Altamira. The music of the Cuna Indians and the spring
of Wolfgang Amadeus Mozart are fraternal messages
which rise from the mystery of the human condition
and ennoble it, and which deserve, like the song of the

nightingale, a place beneath the eternal stars.

Our condition as colonies made us feel, during many years, that European culture was the only one deserving that title. Its arts were the only arts, the proportions of Apollo of Olympia and the marble reflections of Aspasia and Friné the only forms consecrated with beauty. But it also led us to convert into superior models of nature the French gardens and European vegetation, its rivers, its lakes, and its peculiar notion of forests and jungles.

That was fine, as here we had also inherited the language. A language is a tradition, and the universe which flowered in our mouths did not correspond to the universe which girded our hips. Thus, Miguel Antonio Caro wrote elegies to Virgil, Olmedo wrote epic poems in Latin, José María Eguren wove poetry in Verlaine's image in Peru, Banchs envisioned impossible nightingales in Argentina, and even Rubén Darío, the liberator, had divine *marqueses* passing through the thickets of Gautier. Even to this degree, we were a kind of pariah of Europe, exiled offspring stunted by nostalgia, incapable of seeing the world, incapable of being what we were.

The European would say that these illnesses are ours, that it has been years since they participated in this masquerade of Parnassus, and that they do not try to impose the cult of Europe. But their mental order is inscribed in the very structure of Western civilization. Nobody is ignorant of the fact that European pride no longer needs to impose itself with cannons and bombs, because they exhausted their ammunition on the bodies of the Sioux and notched their swords on the flanks of the Aztecs; they left the Caribbean stinking of gunpowder and erased the Araucos. On the skin of India you can also read the signature of English sabers, and on the pyramids, text written by Roman swords; the nose of the Sphinx was blown off by a Napoleonic cannon. European superiority was written in blood and fire over the nations, and the process of recuperation of our conscience has been slow.

Joseph Conrad, at the beginning of our century, portrayed in *Heart of Darkness* the spiritual background of colonialism, the dread which is agitated in the heart by this powerful will to dominate that still threatens to erase humanity.

But it is wise to recall that this proud contempt with which Europe often regards the world is the same manner in which it often regards its various parts — to recall that it is not only a danger for others but a danger to itself. Being a German Nazi meant not only threatening humankind, but threatening the French and the Polish first; being a French nationalist doesn't mean only hating the African *pieds-noirs* but also the Italians and the Spaniards. These ferocious fundamentalisms are like the drowned soldiers of Victor Hugo, who still gnaw at the ropes of their own shipwreck even after sinking to the ocean floor. This mental narrowness is not only found in the hate with which German skinheads kill young Turks, among the French fanatics who profane Jewish cemeteries, and among the Spanish extremists who look contemptuously at Latin Americans; it is also found in the pleasure with which Europeans living slightly more toward the north are in the habit of joking that Africa starts at the Pyrenées. But this attitude, traditionally considered an attack, is more like a form of praise. A certain form of the hegemonic European spirit sees something distinct in Spain, something which doesn't seem to pertain fully to the European tradition. And it doesn't refer especially to poverty, for Greece is roughly equivalent in its poverty. It doesn't refer to a lack of traditions, for Spain was the greatest empire in the world, and its territory gave birth to several Roman emperors. But there is something which ties Spain more closely to the elemental world. For many years I saw the lack of a rationalist tradition in Spain as a historical defect; now I see it as a virtue. It is interesting that Spain has produced not only priests, like the rest of Europe, but also mystics — beings who, as Estanislao Zuleta would put it, establish a personal relationship with the divinity and can dispense with the vast church bureaucracy. While the rest of Europe advanced toward rationalism, and toward what today has become the empire of science, technology and industry — which occurred simultaneously with the onerous triumph of the counterreformation and the absolute submission to the power of Loyola and the Pope — in Spain, something necessary, and possibly promised, to the future took refuge in passion, in loyalty, in hospitality, and (if you like) in insanity. The arrival of utilitarianism and the kingdom of businessmen had buried our age of heroism, magic, faith in miracles, abnegation, and detachment. The relationship between salesman and purchaser arrived to attenuate or erase the ancient miracle of friendship. Friendship, in which there is neither *mine* nor *yours*, that passion which doesn't fit into the universe of the marketplace, is the substance of the book with which the Spanish spirit announced the arrival of the age of greed, and deplored it — and proposed, in contrast to the calculations and securities of reason, the lunacies and generosities of heroism. Facing the temptation of rationalism, now uncontainable, Spain proposed as a discourse and a symbol, folly, delirium, fantasy and friendship: the sublime journey of Sancho and Don Quixote.

It is thus that Spain both is and is not European. It is not the country of the sciences, but the country of the arts. The virtues of its people are not principally those of knowledge, but those of ethics. But ethics will be the only door to enter the future, and maybe we will yet learn from our Spanish heritage how to live without duplicity, how to live with a bit more passion, with a bit more innocence.

Does the rest of Europe lack similar virtues? Surely not. But the illustrious values upon which modernity was founded sustain the hegemonic edifice of this civilization, and have been exalted as the obligatory vir-

tues of humanity. They have brought Nietzsche himself
to assure the species, "You will be consumed by your
virtues." We must encounter different virtues, and not
become so arrogant about them, if we want to escape
from the deafening and bewildering labyrinth of industrial society in whose corners lurks an omnipotent monster with the body of a hydra, an electronic brain, and
an as-yet-undisclosed name.

Today the city — exalted in the West as the frontier
between order and chaos, the refuge against nature,
the museum of immobile yesterdays, the jeweler of
human inventions, and the murmurous hive of reason
— has converted itself into what Henry Miller called "a
nightmare with air conditioning." It is beginning to choke
on its own noxious mists and each day is less capable of
dealing with its own garbage and rubble. And once
again we who are the direct heirs of this tradition are
the first to suffer from the evils which it carries in its
entrails. Looking at Manhattan from the other shore of
the Hudson, the heart is filled with wonder, astonished
by the magnitude of the works of man. We are confronted by this geometric mountain range, this wall
whose parapets want to perforate the heavens in the
style of Babel, and we feel not only its beauty, but also
its fragility. Didn't Rilke say that the beautiful is no
more than a form of the terrible which we are still able
to tolerate? But when we look at Mexico City, ante-
chamber of the infinite city, now almost incapable of
looking at itself; at Medellín, besieged by the violence

of the excluded, assailed nightly by gunshots which ring from hill to hill; at Caracas, designed and built for cars; at Rio, where the hunters of street children lurk in the darkness, we unequivocally see a different vista. All around us we see unemployment, poverty, violence, and helplessness, and we feel that the heritage of civilization has not been generous with the peoples of this side of the world. With the riches of America, Europe reinforced its hegemony; they made the machines and laboratories function. Only thanks to these riches did reason triumph in the West.

But all the virtues of Europe arrived here stripped of their pleasant masks. The Catholic religion, the heart of ambiguous European humanism, arrived destroying the native gods, stripping this grand natural world of its American mythology, and trying in vain to subject its immensities and its abysses to the illusion of a power with a human face. The language, which only modernism has made American, for centuries kept us floating above reality without taking root in it. Even the arts and letters were shown to us not as great examples of the human spirit, but as the only paths of culture. Europe was our teacher and our guide, but it would also be our judge and our conscience. We needed to exhibit in Europe, triumph in Europe, be famous in Europe, earn the indulgence of its wise men, or win the Nobel Prize. We needed to adopt the Universal Declaration of Human and Civil Rights, install the division of public powers, institute universal suffrage, think in European, breathe in European, and not invent anything. But behind Santa Barbara, Changó continued breathing. Beneath the ostentatious standards which allow our governments to confuse the art of governing with the mockery of issuing decrees (always burdensome and usually useless), the people chose the prudent path of pragmatism. Confronted with the infinite spiral of procedures, even the functionaries cheated. Before the imposition of models which have always declared them inferior, trivial, and barbarous, it is not surprising that these people respond with disdain and irreverence. Why should I venerate an order which negates me and relegates me to the last place on the human ladder? Why should I venerate a culture and arts which are offered to me as the patrimony of superior beings, and before which I am denied the right to develop an opinion and even to have feelings? "Treat them as human and they will be human," Goethe said.

I believe that the hour has arrived for the citizens of Latin America to take possession of our world. We should listen to the beautiful words of Robert Frost:

Something we were withholding made us weak,
Until we found out that it was ourselves
We were withholding from our land of living,
And forthwith found salvation in surrender.

Do we know the names of the trees that accompany us on this mysterious adventure? It is not enough, I believe, to protect them from the plundering of insatiable industry; we also need to know them and love them. Do we know the astounding variety of creatures who are, like us, children of this territory? Aren't the mockingbirds and the armadillos, the frogs and the butterflies, our responsibility? We now know that man cannot destroy everything without destroying himself; we must also realize that man cannot save himself without saving everything. Maybe we will be obliged to change the Declaration of Human Rights to a Declaration of Universal Rights of the World, of which mankind is but a tiny and dangerous fraction. We are — like all the peoples that now are and ever have been — in the center of the world, and it is indispensable that we become conscious of that.

I think we will also need to invent institutions which correspond to us. We must forget the failed structure of these useless States which demand everything and give nothing back in exchange, which corrupt every heart that devotes itself to them, and which govern with decrees based on statistics and feel nothing before the prostration, the helplessness and the agony of millions of human beings. "Before the dangers of totalitarianism," said Borges, "maybe our poor individualism could still play a role. Aren't all the traditions and all the races here? Don't all the dreams and longings of the planet converge in our valleys?" Nobody has known better than Borges how to present the wealth of this borderline position between the Western cultural tradition (which belongs to us naturally), the tradition of the whole world, and the mysteries of our American being. He was wise enough to tell us that the death of an old friend in Buenos Aires was equal to the death of Caesar. He was wise enough to tell us, evoking Evaristo Carriego, that our world was as deserving as any other of poetry and history. He told us, remembering Heraclitus of Ephesus whom some visitors had surprised in the kitchen, "Enter, the gods are here as well." He dedicated his entire life, his astounding talent and his profound erudition to showing us that here also can reality be found in all its plenitude. He insisted that the theater of our life and our death must be honored; that our poetry must speak of our territory, that "...Here also is that unknown, and anxious and brief thing, life..."; that here, on any streetcorner of Guayaquil or Valencia, of Santiago or Managua, on any shore of the Parana or the Orinoco, on any street in Matanzas or Lima, on any ranch in Magdalena or Chaco, in any boarding house in Veracruz, in any basement in Buenos Aires, we can find the *Aleph*, the universe. And from Borges we have also learned the secret of serene humility, the certainty that everyone who knows he has a thing which will inevitably be lost, doesn't need to resort to imposition. Our only possible chance for greatness will be through identifying ourselves with the causes of the world, far from every stingy local pride, and not constructing for ourselves paradigms of any kind of superiority. Neither richness nor knowledge, neither

force nor tradition, can be instruments to exclude or
silence the others. Before the overbearing need to save
not only the future, today vastly threatened, but also
everything which seemed definitive — the yesterdays,
the dead, and the myths — even the most minimal and
tenuous knowledge of the eternally silent and excluded
peoples must be heard like the voice of God himself. It
is enough to glance at the vital riches of the peoples of
Africa and the native peoples of America — magically
forged to nature, friendly with the forests and the rocks
— and compare them to these formidable and terrible
hives which our pride has erected, to understand that
there is a twisted knowledge; to see that some keys to
open the future have been ignored only because they
were discovered by the meek — because they weren't
dictated by greed or the will to dominate, but by cordiality, respect, reverence, and other virtues which, like
a certain magical personality of our literature, "...doesn't
want to be correct in a triumphal way." They are wis-
doms of the meek — but despite the nuclear arsenals,
the pollution, the armies of technology, the oceans of
plastic, despite the infinite power which sits like an
ominous cloud on the horizon of civilization, maybe
man or God wasn't completely wrong when he declared
that the meek shall inherit the earth.

Today it is an urgent necessity that we acquire or
recuperate a consciousness that the world is much more
vast and much richer than the reductive chorus of capital
would like to have us think. Restored to its true propor-

tions, European culture will let us hear the buzz of other cultures: the musicians who refuse to impose themselves through the electronic pandemonium; the art which does not feel obliged to pass through the ever more problematic filter of European and North American galleries; the literatures which do not try to make their paths through the lies of advertising and marketing; the examples of symbiosis between distinct races and traditions; the study of the innumerable dialects and languages of the nations, villages and tribes who don't intend to impose them as superior languages; the persistence of legends. And we must redouble our efforts not to fall into the dominating and condescending habits of the Western tradition. Someday we will have said farewell to that intolerant world of *conquistadors* and evangelizers, who are masters of the truth because they are masters of the sword, and who erect their inventions, undoubtedly admirable, as the exclusive forms of beauty, truth and good.

We can criticize Europe and its inventions because we are Europeans, but especially because its destiny is important to us. We, too, carry the legacy of tribal hatred; but here there is such a great diversity of races and peoples, of religions and superstitions, and the cross-breeding and combination are so great that after five centuries the rivers of our blood lines have merged, and it is very difficult for these hatreds to prosper. As long as we don't become drunk on pride or hostility, as long as we don't try to negate others, local cultures will be a defense against the obscene uniformization of the planet. Here the devil of nationalism is also active, but the brotherhood of traditions and the common treasure of language could serve us well as an antidote. The truth is that in this critical and nostalgic mode we are Europeans. We are also feeling the growing pulse of a continental fraternity only beginning to be contradicted by the formalism of the governments and the suspicions of the armies — who with good reason fear that the cordiality between nations will emasculate them into decorative and useless bodies.

Hate still has its refuges. But it is our duty to add to the current of the rich and powerful planetary tradition all that we have and still are not even aware of, all that which — due to hegemonic Western thinking — we have not known how to value.

An active Europe stretched itself out to all the corners of the world, but I suspect it did not know how to see much of them. Thus it melted exquisite works of art into ingots, sacked sacred tombs to stock its museums, destroyed temples to take possession of their divine reliquaries, or tore up stone pillars full of inscriptions that an antique culture knew how to conceive and construct, only to make them the centers of some soulless plazas. Thus it reduced to silence and indifference dreams and traditions that weren't accidental forms of human inventiveness, but indispensable secrets for the survival of the species.

It is still necessary to investigate what the world has

been deprived of to date — what has been silenced by the sackings of greed and the uproar of arrogance. It is still necessary to say that the people who died defending themselves have left behind a scream which waits in the throats of the living. Before the lethal cloud which advances over the world — full of knowledge, power, technology, products, advertising, spectacles which immobilize mankind and incomprehensible atomic arsenals — before this lavish and admirable power that denies the sacred and plunders nature and all the profane, we continue to have only one power to oppose, the last sanctuary of hope: the power of the divine, a force waiting in the form of dreams and legends, in friendship and in love, in art and in memory, in perplexity and in gratitude, in the hearts of human beings. That force will never appear in any statistic, and thus doesn't seem to exist nor count before the evident powers of chaos, but is still that which built the nations, invented the languages, refined the trades, and knew how to raise up in serenade, under the significant stars, the only truly dignified thing which has sometimes sprouted from our lips and our hands: the respectful song of gratitude and hope.

about the author

WILLIAM OSPINA was born in Padua, Tolima, in the Colombian Andes, in March of 1954. He was raised in different towns throughout the mountains. He studied law at the Universidad Santiago in Cali, and subsequently worked as a journalist and publicist in Cali and Bogotá. He lived in Europe between 1979 and 1982. Upon his return to Colombia he won a national essay prize for a work about the Colombian author Aurelio Arturo, and began his career as an independent writer. He has represented Colombia in literary competitions in Quebec and Mexico, and visited the U.S. in 1990, 1991 and 1992. He has published three books of poems: *Hilo de Arena* (1986); *La Luna del Dragón* (1992); and *El País del Viento* (1992), which won the National Poetry Prize. He has also published four books of essays: *Aurelio Arturo* (1991), *Es Tarde Para El Hombre* (1994), *Esos Estraños Prófugos de Occidente* (1994), and *Un Algebra Embrujada* (1995). Additionally, he has translated *Tres Cuentos* by Gustave Flaubert. He has taught literature seminars at the Universidad del Valle, the Universidad de los Andes, and the Universidad National de Colombia. He is currently preparing his fourth book of poems, *¿Con Quien Habla Virginia Caminando Hacia El Agua?*, and a new book of essays, *La Edad de los Diojes Ausentes*. He lives in Bogotá, Colombia.

Witch
crone